THE PRINCE OF VENICE BEACH

BY BLAKE NELSON

LITTLE, BROWN AND COMPANY

NEW YORK   BOSTON

Copyright © 2014 by Blake Nelson

Map © Shutterstock, Globe Turner

Little, Brown and Company

Hachette Book Group
237 Park Avenue, New York, NY 10017
Visit our website at lb-teens.com

Little, Brown and Company is a division of Hachette Book Group, Inc.
The Little, Brown name and logo are trademarks of Hachette Book Group, Inc.

The publisher is not responsible for websites (or their content)
that are not owned by the publisher.

First Edition: June 2014

Library of Congress Cataloging-in-Publication Data

Nelson, Blake
  The prince of Venice Beach / by Blake Nelson.—First edition.
    pages cm
  Summary: Robert "Cali" Callahan, seventeen, gets swept into the private-investigator business and must deal with the ramifications of looking for fellow runaways who may not want to be found—and with falling in love with one of them.
  ISBN 978-0-316-23048-3 (hardcover)—ISBN 978-0-316-23047-6 (e-book)
  [1. Runaways—Fiction. 2. Homeless persons—Fiction. 3. Private investigators—Fiction. 4. Venice (Los Angeles, Calif.)—Fiction.] I. Title.
  PZ7.N4328Pri 2014
  [Fic]—dc23
                                                                    2013012248

10 9 8 7 6 5 4 3 2 1

RRD-C

Printed in the United States of America

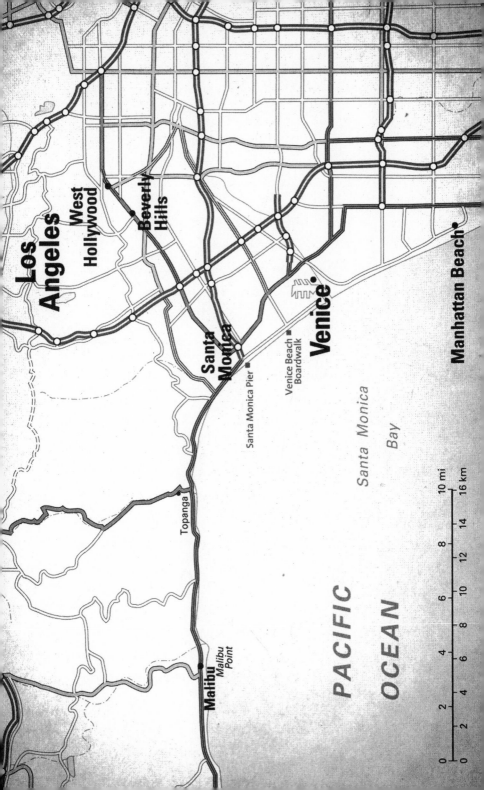

ONE

They came from Minnesota and you could tell by the way they walked onto the court that they'd heard about Venice street ball. This was the big time, and they wanted to try their luck, to test themselves, to see how their midwestern white-boy game measured up in the palm-tree jungle of Southern California.

They were tall, with big shoulders and straight white teeth in their farm-boy faces. You could feel that midwestern pride, you could sense their focus and competitive spirit. *For God and country and apple pie.* Their unselfish, "team-first" approach probably won them the high school championship up in Lake Nahaka or Dingle Falls or wherever they came from. Ol' Coach Wankershank up there had taught them how to compete like men, how to buckle down and play defense and control the paint.

Now they found themselves on the legendary street-basketball courts of Venice Beach. Their first opponents of the day being: me, five feet nine, surfer white-boy, in old Vans and cutoffs...Jojo Hendrix, five feet eight, homeless and quite fragrant black dude of unknown age or origin... and Diego Rodriguez, six feet one, 235 pounds, the "Mountain of Mexican," who had just turned fifteen, and who desperately needed a belt to hold up his pants.

This was gonna be fun. Even the guys on the other courts could see what was coming. They gathered around to watch.

The Minnesota boys took the ball out first. They ran a play, a cross screen. One guy blocked out Diego; the other guy cut to the hoop. One quick pass and they scored an easy layup.

Jojo smiled and congratulated them. That's because Jojo loves everyone and wants each of us to self-realize and be the best person he can be, and also to find Jesus Christ if possible and be saved by his love, and ultimately disconnect from all this earthly stuff, like money and pride and even basketball. Jojo is like that, full of love and forgiveness and the Lord. He'd give you his last quarter, except he probably already gave it to somebody else.

The Minnesota boys were unsure how to respond to Jojo. They maintained their focus. They took the ball out again and ran a different play and got another layup. I suggested to

Diego that he move toward the middle, because he's big and strong and unmovable, and at least they wouldn't get any more easy buckets.

The Minnesotans countered this strategy by shooting jump shots. With their practiced technique and perfect ball rotation, they hit four in a row. Jojo, meanwhile, was busy telling someone in the bleachers how beautiful a day it was, how it was "God's day." Diego, on his side of the court, struggled to hold up his pants.

It was 7–0 when they finally missed a shot. Diego wrestled away the rebound. He passed it to me. I passed it to Jojo. He passed it back. The Minnesota boys positioned themselves to play defense. They were grinning to each another, thrilled with how well this was going. They weren't just beating the locals, they were *dominating*. They tugged on the bottoms of their shorts and adjusted their sweatbands. You wondered if they wanted it to be harder. There was almost a feeling of letdown, of this being too easy.

"Jojo," I said, passing the ball back to him. "We're behind. We need to score."

So Jojo snapped out of whatever spiritual experience he was having. He dribbled once, sliced through the Minnesota boys, and elevated over everyone. The ball rolled off his fingers and into the hoop.

The boys' mouths fell open. *Where did that come from?*

They exchanged looks of wonder, but before they could react, I'd checked the ball and shot a bullet pass to Jojo, who was already in the lane. He went airborne and dunked it, right over their tallest guy.

That's right, he *dunked* it.

We took it out again. I passed it to Jojo, and in a blur of quickness he knifed through their defense, hung in the air for an impossible amount of time, and laid it in the basket.

The boys began looking at each other. How did you stop this? What strategy could they use?

I passed the ball to Jojo again, who faked a drive to the basket. All three Minnesotans scrambled backward in wild panic, two of them falling on their asses on the concrete.

Jojo stared at them a moment, refocused on the hoop, and shot an effortless jumper. *Swish.*

The local guys were cracking up. Someone in the bleachers offered directions back to Minnesota. Other comments were slightly racist but also pretty funny. The white boys were trying. They were learning. They'd had the *cojones* to come down here at least, you had to give them credit.

I passed the ball to Jojo again, who slipped a perfect underneath pass to Diego, who gently bounced the ball off the backboard and into the hoop.

Then I shot a jumper and made it. Then Jojo shot a jumper and made it. Then a quick pass to Diego and now we were the ones getting the easy layups.

The Minnesota boys stood staring at us in shock. They had never seen someone like Jojo up close. His talent level is, I would guess, somewhere around NBA starting point guard.

Sure, he spent most of his time giving praise to the Lord or communing with the angels on a higher plane, but when he did come down to earth, he had special powers: mainly the ability to fly.

Jojo dunked on the Minnesota boys one last time to end the game. The three of them stood, baffled and humiliated in the middle of the court. A new team came on to replace them. There were no kind words. No one complimented them or said "good game." This wasn't the YMCA.

Still, their best guy came toward me. He was gonna say something, shake hands, whatever. But I just nodded like: Don't say a word. You guys showed us what you got, and it wasn't bad. Really, you did all right. But whatever little suburban bubble you live in is just that, a bubble. This is Venice. This is the real stuff.

Later, though, I did shake his hand. I guess I have that midwestern sense of honor in me too. Guys like that, I look at them and I can't help but think: *That could have been me....*

TWO

By noon, it was too hot to play. People wandered off. Diego and I stood around, lazily shooting jump shots in the sun. That's when I noticed a guy standing at the edge of the court. He wore sunglasses and a coat and tie. It was an odd look in a place where most people wore board shorts and flip-flops.

Diego shot some free throws. I stood under the basket and tossed the ball back to him. I watched the guy. He was looking for someone. He kept checking out different people on the courts.

Then he settled on me.

He waited until I went to the drinking fountain and casually strolled over. "Excuse me," he said. "I'm looking for a young man named Cali."

I glanced up at him but said nothing. He'd have to take the sunglasses off if he wanted to talk to me.

I went back to the water, which tasted like chlorine. You needed bottled water down here, but that cost money.

He took off his glasses. I straightened up and wiped the water off my chin with the back of my wrist. "What do you want him for?" I asked.

"I need help finding someone."

I followed him back to his car. He pulled some papers out of a briefcase and spread them on the hood.

"This is him," he told me. He handed me a picture of a high school kid, probably seventeen. He looked like the Minnesota boys: clean, suburban, straight teeth. In the picture, he was wearing a red hoodie and a baseball cap hanging sideways off his head.

I didn't look very long, just a glance, really. I handed back the picture.

"And you are?" I asked the guy.

"My name is Bruce Edwards."

"Why are you looking for him?"

"I'm a private investigator," he answered. He handed me a business card. He also showed me an official-looking photo ID and then reached into his car to get a license from the state of California, which he kept in his glove compartment.

"Who told you about me?" I asked.

"A cop friend. Darius Howard."

I nodded. Darius Howard had busted me when I first got to California. Well, actually, someone else busted me, but I ended up in Detective Howard's office in the Venice precinct. I hadn't done anything, I'd just been stopped on the boardwalk and had no ID.

Darius had understood my situation. I'd been a foster kid my whole life, back in Nebraska. At fourteen, I'd struck out on my own. I'd landed in Venice and made a little life for myself, off the grid, of course. But I was doing okay and I wasn't causing any trouble for the police. So Darius had let me walk.

"His name is Chad Mitchell," said Edwards, showing me some more pictures. "He's from Seattle. Nice family. Good school. According to this, he should be in the area."

He handed me a printout of credit card charges. You could follow it like a trail. Seattle...Seattle...Seattle...then a gas station in Portland, Oregon...a mini-mart in southern Oregon...a gas station in California...food and a motel outside San Francisco...and then Santa Monica, where he'd bought some sandwiches at a grocery store.

His last purchase—a six-pack of Mountain Dew and a bag of Doritos—was from the Beach Mart half a block from where we were standing.

"Darius said you know what goes on down here," said Bruce Edwards. "He thought you might be able to help. There'd be a little money in it for you."

I nodded and looked at the pictures. I could always use a little money.

"His parents are very concerned," said Edwards. "Needless to say."

"All right," I said. "I'll keep my eyes open."

"Let me give you my number," he said, getting out his phone.

I took his number.

Cool as I acted, I was excited for this opportunity. Several months before, Darius Howard had asked for my help in another case, a local kid who stole bicycles. He'd steal them and throw them off the pier for fun. I didn't get paid or anything, but I did help find the kid. Darius had been impressed.

So maybe this could lead to something. A part-time job. Helping find people. I noticed people anyway. It was like a hobby. Especially kids my own age. Tourist kids, surfer kids, homeless kids: I'd check them out. I'd try to guess where they came from, what their deal was.

Ever since the bike stealer, I'd hoped Darius Howard might ask for my help again. And now, in a way, he had.

That afternoon, I cruised on my skateboard up and down the boardwalk, checking in with different people, not asking anything specific, more just dropping the name.

"Dude, this guy Chad's in town...." I said to some local skateboarders. No response.

I told some other people about a Seattle guy named Chad who was gonna buy my surfboard. Had anybody seen him? No one had.

I cruised around. I thought about where I'd gone when I first arrived in Venice. But that didn't help too much. Chad Mitchell had a car, he had money, he wouldn't be sleeping in storm drains like I did.

Still, he had to be somewhere. And he'd bought Doritos at the Beach Mart. It was likely he was close by.

That night, I went home to Hope Stillwell's. She was a local woman who let me live in a treehouse in her backyard. She also let me use her computer sometimes, which was what I did now.

I found Chad Mitchell on Facebook. He seemed like a normal kid. His parents were well-off. He had nice clothes, an amazing bedroom. He liked skateboarding, snowboarding, video games. He'd taken surf lessons on a recent vacation in Hawaii. "Surfing is the *best*," he wrote under a picture of himself, standing awkwardly on a baby wave.

He also liked to party. And goof off. And do what he wanted. "I got a bad attitude!" he wrote under another picture of himself, flipping off a mall security guard whose back was turned.

Since he wanted to be a surfer, I rode the bus to Malibu the next morning and got off at Surfrider Beach. There wasn't much going on, the waves weren't great. Still, there were people out. I watched for anyone with rental boards or taking lessons. I showed the guy at the rental booth a picture of Chad. He hadn't seen him.

I walked down to Malibu Plaza. I checked out the grocery store, the surf shop, the frozen-yogurt place. I showed my picture to some girls who worked at a sunglasses store. Nothing. I rode the bus home and microwaved a burrito and sat in my treehouse and thought about Chad Mitchell. Where did guys like that hang out? What would they do at night?

Before bed, I rode my skateboard the length of the Venice boardwalk. It was dark and quiet, and the homeless people were settling in for the night. They had their dogs, their packs, their shopping carts. Some of them were just starting off their life on the street. They still had decent clothes and clean sleeping pads, and their hair wasn't all gnarly yet. I sniffed around the newer people as best I could.

"You guys from Seattle...?"

"I'm lookin' for my buddy Chad...?"

"Any new people around...?"

But nothing came of it.

The next day, I called Bruce. I told him where I'd been, what I was doing, and asked if anything new had turned up on his end. Nothing had. He seemed impressed with my activity, though, and told me to keep at it. He offered to send me a check for my time and expenses, which I told him to make out to Hope Stillwell.

When the check came, I told Hope to keep it, since she didn't charge me rent. She was psyched and went to Trader Joe's and made a big vegan feast and had a bunch of her woman friends over. Afterward, they had a little dance party in the backyard. They cranked up the music and I danced with Hope's friend Olivia, who's just about the most beautiful woman I've ever seen. She's thirty-two, though, and I'm seventeen, so she just laughs when I try to talk to her. I'm not really on her radar. Hope's friends think of me as a street kid, a charity case. I'm like their pet. I'm their good deed.

On Saturday a new southwest swell came in, so everyone went surfing. I had a new wet suit, which I was eager to try. I'd found it in the alley and cut off the arms and legs a few inches to make it fit.

I grabbed my board from Hope's garage and met Diego at the breakwater. The waves were big and we picked our way out through the gaps in the surf. Diego and I both got up on the same wave. Diego's a good surfer, but he's so big on his tiny board he looks more funny than cool. We started bumping each other, pushing each other, goofing around. But there were so many people I was afraid I was gonna hit someone. Or get hit.

That's a constant fear, when you're off the grid: getting hurt and ending up in the emergency room. Or worse, the dentist. One runaway kid I knew broke a bunch of teeth at the skate park, and while the dentist fixed him up, one of the nurses ran him through a national database.

Two hours later, all Novocained up and with a mouth of fake teeth, he walked into a waiting room full of cops and social services people. That was the end of his ride. Back he went to Pennsylvania.

So I let Diego take the wave and paddled back to the lineup.

THREE

After surfing, I went back to Hope's. I stashed my board and hung up my wet suit to dry. I rinsed the salt and sand out of my hair with the garden hose and then ate a couple oranges.

After that, I skateboarded back to the boardwalk to continue my search for Chad Mitchell. I cruised by the chess tables where Tommy Shirts and some of the older guys were sitting around. I stopped and sat with them and watched the thick crowd of people walking by. Everyone in Venice walks the boardwalk at some point during the day. So it's a good way to see who's around.

Tommy Shirts was telling a story about some recent trouble he'd gotten into with the cops. It was the same story Tommy always told: He was minding his own business, not hurting anybody, not trying to steal anything (Tommy was always trying to steal something), and then some cop comes along and starts harassing him....

I was only half listening. I spun the wheel of my skateboard with my fingers. It was late afternoon now, and hot. I was in the mood for a nap. Or maybe a slice of pizza. I lifted my head up to see who was working at the Pizza Slice...and that's when I saw the kid.

My eyes went right to him, despite the crowd. He was by himself, on foot. I didn't see his face, but there was something about him. He had a strange energy. He wore red shorts and brand-new sneakers, but he also seemed a little ragged, a little out of sorts.

And his hair: That was the giveaway. He had rich-kid hair, layered and wavy, no sideburns, a real professional cut.

I kept my eyes on him as he moved along. Then I eased away from Tommy Shirts and his endless cop stories.

I hopped on my skateboard and slowly coasted along behind the guy, staying about twenty yards back.

He didn't seem too comfortable on the crowded boardwalk. Some local skateboarders sped by, weaving wildly through the tourists. He had to jump out of the way. Then he cursed them and flipped them off after they'd passed.

He was definitely not from around here.

He walked farther and then turned up one of the side streets. I let him go, staying on the boardwalk but keeping him in sight.

He walked up the hill, then pulled out a set of keys and

beeped open a car. It was a blue Volvo, pretty new. It had ski racks. The plates were from Washington State.

I stayed where I was. I watched him get in the car. I couldn't see what he was doing inside. I assumed the car would drive off, but it didn't. It stayed parked where it was.

I decided to do a walk-by. I picked up my board and walked casually up the hill, right toward the Volvo. As I approached, I could see the obvious signs of someone living in their car. A bathing suit laid out to dry in the back window. Fast-food cups, hamburger wrappers. Rumpled clothes piled in the backseat. A crinkled map. As I passed, I glanced down and saw his face full on. It was definitely him. Chad Mitchell. He was just sitting there, bored. He was playing with the thick gold watch on his wrist.

When I was a block beyond the car, I casually stepped into a doorway and ducked out of sight. I called Bruce Edwards.

"I found him," I said.

"Where is he?"

"Sitting in a car on Rose Avenue. Just up from the board-walk." I told Edwards the license plate number.

He wrote it down. "How's he look?" he asked.

"Fine. Far as I can tell."

"All right, stay with him. I'll call the parents and see how they want to proceed."

I hung up. I stood in the doorway, balancing the nose of my skateboard on the top of my foot. There was a lot of pedestrian traffic on the street. Mostly people coming back from the beach. A few going the other direction. I felt pretty invisible standing there. Nobody notices a kid with a skateboard. Except maybe another kid.

After about five minutes, Chad Mitchell got out of his car. I checked my phone—no word yet from Bruce.

Chad opened his trunk and got out a skateboard, an expensive longboard, brand-new from the looks of it. He shut the trunk and locked the car with the remote.

I stayed out of sight.

He headed down the hill toward the boardwalk, walking at first and then getting on his longboard. I stepped out of the doorway and followed.

It was evening now. The sun was going down. The crowd on the boardwalk had thinned out. Chad cruised on his longboard, pushing lightly, then coasting for long stretches. I cruised too, staying with him. With fewer people around, it was harder to stay out of sight, to stay inconspicuous. I had to hang back, pushing slowly against the concrete, my older, crappier board rattling along in the growing darkness.

Chad Mitchell wasn't much of a skateboarder, but his fancy board made up for it. It seemed to push itself, that's how smooth it rolled. He had skate shoes I'd never seen before, made of some hemp weave, it looked like. Maybe that was a rich-kid thing, or the latest trend in Seattle.

He rolled along. I got the sense, even from far behind him, that he wasn't having much fun. He'd probably enjoyed his new freedom for the first couple days. Away from authority, from teachers and parents. But then the freedom gets to you. And the isolation. No family. No friends. Not even a dog. How many times can you go to McDonald's and eat cheeseburgers by yourself? How many days can you spend on the beach? How many nights can you sleep in your car?

Not as many as you think.

Then something unexpected happened. Two guys appeared. They were a little ahead of us, and on foot, but I could see they had locked onto Chad. They must have spotted the longboard and known how expensive it was. They'd also sized up Chad and could see how little resistance he'd put up.

They didn't hesitate. One of them charged across the boardwalk and body-slammed him from the side. Chad went flying and hit the concrete with a heavy thud. One of the guys grabbed the board and then they both swarmed over Chad.

I started to run forward, then stopped myself. *No*, I thought. *Better to let nature run its course.*

I hung back and blended with the dozen or so tourists who had stopped to gawk at this sudden violence. The first guy grabbed Chad by his shirtfront, lifted him off the ground, and punched him in the face.

That was hard to watch.

The other guy yanked Chad's hemp-weave shoes off his feet. This was also hard to watch. But I stayed where I was.

They went through Chad's pockets. It happened so fast the people standing there barely had time to register what was happening.

I glanced behind me and saw a police car crawling along the boardwalk about a quarter-mile away. The cops couldn't see what was happening here yet. But things could get complicated if they did.

Chad, from the ground, made a feeble attempt to kick his attackers. They punched him in the face again. This time, the side of Chad's head bounced hard off the pavement.

"Where's my weed!?" said the guy loudly. This was apparently to fool onlookers into thinking this was a drug deal gone bad. It was a good strategy. Nobody wanted to get involved in a drug deal. It totally worked. Everyone moved back a step.

The second guy found Chad's wallet, attached to a wallet chain, which he tore off Chad's belt loop with one yank.

I always knew those chains were useless.

The last thing they took was Chad's thick gold watch, which they pulled off his wrist. I glanced behind me to check on the police car, and when I turned back the two thieves were gone. They were that fast.

The growing crowd now moved toward Chad. He was lying on his side, bleeding and crying and groaning in pain. His white athletic socks, half pulled off, looked strangely clean and ordinary in this otherwise miserable scene.

I couldn't let the cops get him. I stepped forward. A tourist woman was leaning over Chad, inspecting his face. I pushed her away.

"Chad? Chad Mitchell?" I said.

Chad opened his eyes and stared up at me.

"Dude, the cops are coming," I said. "We gotta go."

"But he's hurt!" said a tourist.

"Don't move his neck!" said a woman.

"Back off!" I barked, and the tourists moved quickly away.

An old man saw the squad car in the distance. "Look!" he cried. "The police! Someone call them!" People started waving their arms.

I pulled Chad to his feet. He couldn't straighten up, but I got him moving, steering him away from the tourists, up a side street, and down an alley. We hid behind a Dumpster.

Crouched on the ground, Chad groaned and held his ribs. Then he felt the blood on his chin. "What the—!?" he said, touching his lips. "I'm bleeding! My whole mouth is bleeding!"

I found a napkin on the ground and handed it to him. "Dude, you're fine. You're okay." I peeked over the Dumpster and checked to see where the squad car was.

"They took my wallet!" Chad cried suddenly. He was feeling around in his empty pockets. "And my keys! Where are my keys? They took my car keys!"

I told him to stay quiet and stay down. He did, and the cop car passed without seeing us.

When Chad realized he had been totally cleaned out, he lowered his swollen face into his knees and started to sob.

I sat there with him, not comforting him, just letting him cry. "Some other creep tried to rob me yesterday," he moaned. "What's wrong with these people? This is supposed to be the beach! This is supposed to be fun!"

"You're easy money," I said.

The truth of this made him cry more, which I figured was probably good.

I let several minutes go by. I waited until he'd cried himself out.

"What are you going to do now?" I finally asked him.

"I just wanna go home," he said into his knees. "I just wanna go back to Seattle. I hate it here. This place sucks!"

"You sure about that?"

"Of course I'm sure!" he whined.

"Okay," I said quietly. I got out my phone. I called Bruce Edwards.

"I'm sitting here with Chad," I told him. "He says he wants to go home."

"Good work," said Bruce.

FOUR

Hope Stillwell was singing in the backyard when I woke up the next morning. She did that sometimes while she hung up her sheets on the clothesline. I was in the treehouse and I rolled over and watched her. Hope did a lot of things like that: singing, doing yoga, getting up early to work in her garden. She was a pretty happy person in general. I felt pretty good too. I felt pretty great. I had found Chad Mitchell. And sent him home to his parents in one piece.

I ate an orange for breakfast and headed down toward the beach. I cruised along the boardwalk like I owned the place. When I first came to Venice, I was so clueless. I couldn't skate, I couldn't surf, I didn't know what *gnarly* meant. People called me "Cali" or "California" as a joke. But now I really was "California," maybe more than a lot of people.

I cruised by the basketball courts. Huge Diego was there on his tiny BMX bike. That was always an amusing sight. We got a game going with some older dudes, some weekend-warrior types. All through the game, though, I kept looking over at the drinking fountain where Bruce Edwards had appeared. Would he want to hire me again? I had definitely come through for him. Could I work for him on a regular basis somehow? Or maybe become a private investigator myself someday? It seemed possible.

That night, Hope was having one of her knitting circles, so it was crowded in the house: a dozen women, chattering away, yarn balls rolling around on the floor, cats. I grabbed some snacks and headed to my treehouse. Hope had turned on the Christmas lights and the Chinese lanterns in the backyard, so there was a nice glow back there. I balanced my can of Pepsi on a plate of chips and salsa and climbed my ladder one-handed.

I got settled and turned on my radio. Usually at night, I listened to the Lakers game or *Coast to Coast*, which is a talk show about paranormal activity and UFOs. Tonight, though, I tuned it to a classical station. I did that because I was thinking about my possible future as a private investigator. I was worried I wasn't cultured enough. Chad Mitchell was a rich kid. Which meant his parents probably went to the opera or the symphony or whatever. You probably needed to know certain things to work for people like that. And act a certain way. That was why Bruce Edwards wore a coat and tie, even at the beach. You had to look professional.

I pictured myself, years from now, being like Bruce Edwards: coat and tie, official business cards, a license from the state of California.

I imagined my own picture ID:

ROBERT "CALI" CALLAHAN
PRIVATE INVESTIGATOR

In the picture, I would look tough and unflinching. I imagined being in a hotel lounge somewhere and someone asking me what I did for a living. At first, I'd avoid the subject, I'd be vague. But if they kept after me, I'd show them my ID.

"You're a private detective?" they'd say, amazed. "Do you carry a gun?"

"I don't need a gun," I'd say.

I liked the sound of that. Maybe I'd put that on my business card:

ROBERT "CALI" CALLAHAN
PRIVATE INVESTIGATOR
"I DON'T NEED A GUN."

Or maybe I'd just get a gun. I'd have to take a gun class anyway, at some point. And I'd have to go to a shooting range. I pictured myself with the earmuffs, the safety glasses, blasting away when the cardboard bad guy spun in my direction: *Blam blam blam blam—*

"Cali?" said a voice from below. I snapped out of my daydream and looked down. It was Ailis, a nerdy girl who hung out with Hope and her friends sometimes. She must have been at the knitting circle.

"Hey, Ailis," I said.

"Hey," she said back. "What are you doing?"

"Nothing. Getting ready for bed."

"Is that classical music you're listening to?"

I should have known that somehow, some way, somebody was going to give me crap about the classical music.

"Yes, it is, Ailis. Do you have a problem with that?"

"No. I just find it interesting that you, who lives in a treehouse and barely knows how to read, are listening to something so sophisticated."

"I know how to read, Ailis," I said to her. "I happen to be reading *War and Peace* at the moment."

This was sort of true. I had an old paperback copy of *War and Peace.* A hobo I'd met had torn the book in half and given me the front half. I'd never read it, though. But I was going to, as part of my new plan to educate myself.

"Do you even know what composer this is?"

"No, I don't, Ailis." I lay back the way I was, staring upward, imagining my private-investigator badge.

"I think it's Mozart," said Ailis. "But I could be wrong."

"I don't really care," I said to my treehouse ceiling. "I don't even like it, to tell you the truth. I was just giving it a try."

"I think that's very admirable."

"Thank you, Ailis. Is there anything else?"

There was a long silence from down in the yard. I wondered if she'd gone back inside. I rolled over and looked.

She was still there. She swallowed nervously and said, "Hope said you might want to see *Battle for Santa Cruz*."

This was true. *Battle for Santa Cruz* was a new movie about an alien invasion of California. That was my favorite type of movie, and I definitely wanted to see it. And now, thanks to Chad Mitchell, I had some money. I would probably go see *Battle for Santa Cruz* that week.

"Yeah," I said. "I'll probably see it."

"Do you want to go together? It's playing at the Nuart."

"Are you asking me out on a date, Ailis?" I said.

"No, I'm just saying if we both want to see it, we could go together. It's weird for girls to go to movies by themselves. I never got to see the last Harry Potter movie."

"Go with Hope," I said.

"Hope's too old. She doesn't like alien-invasion movies."

"Well, go with someone your own age, then."

"You are my own age."

I stared down at Ailis. She had thick black hair and was lately wearing big black glasses, which gave her a dorky, robotic look. Which was fine except that she was eighteen, which was a little old for the robot-nerd thing. Like, that would be funny if she were ten. But she was out of high school. She actually went to Santa Monica Community College. She shouldn't be so weird and computer-like and into Harry Potter movies. But then, if she were normal, she would have normal guys taking her to the movies and she wouldn't be bothering me.

"All right, Ailis. When do you want to go?"

"Tuesday?"

"Okay."

She turned and walked away. Then she stopped halfway across the yard and turned back. She pushed her glasses up her nose. "Thank you for going with me," she said.

"Okay, Ailis."

The next day, at the basketball courts, I ended up on a team playing *against* Jojo Hendrix. Even worse, I actually had to guard him. This was deeply humbling but also fun, if you like a challenge. It wasn't totally impossible to guard Jojo. You just had to account for his superhuman speed and quickness. Also it helped if you talked to him and got him thinking about other things. Like, what language did God speak? English? Spanish? Chinese? And how small were angels? The size of a small person or a small pet or a dime or a molecule?

The other fun part of playing in a Jojo game was that people would come watch. He was that electric. One or two spectacular plays and a ripple would spread out across the boardwalk. People could sense something amazing was happening. They wouldn't know where it was at first. They'd start looking around, checking the street performers, looking out toward the beach. Then they'd realize: *It's coming from the basketball courts.*

Sometimes a hundred people would gather around the court to watch Jojo. Dudes were always telling him, "You should charge admission." Or someone would offer to pass the hat or whatever, let the people show their appreciation and get Jojo a couple bucks, maybe even enough to buy him a decent meal or a pair of real basketball shoes. But that wasn't his thing; he wasn't interested in that. "I don't need nothing," he would say, "as long as I am able to love God." That was a little weird for most people. So they'd shut up and let Jojo get back to the game.

After an hour of getting humiliated on the basketball court, I went to the outdoor showers to wash off. In general, I tried to take care of my personal hygiene before I went back to Hope's house, since she only had one bathroom and there were often other people staying there too, women passing through, people protesting something, or once this lady who was living in her car in the driveway. I wasn't the only person Hope helped out.

So I waited my turn and got under the outdoor shower, with my shorts and my T-shirt still on. I found some soap someone had left, which I used to clean my shirt. Then I rubbed it around inside my pants. The tourists stared at me like they do, but that's the fun of living at the beach. You've always got an audience. There's was always some dude from Denmark or some lady from Canada taking your picture and saying to her husband, "Look how the beach people live!" Sometimes they want to talk to you and hear what goes on. "Do you really not go to school?" this girl asked me once. She was from Portugal. I walked her out to the pier to watch the fishermen. She said it reminded her of home. I was like, what? She said Portugal was right on the ocean, it was just like California. I was pretty sure Portugal was closer to Russia. But I didn't know for sure. That was another example of ways I needed to educate myself. In my mind I started a list:

- *Learn about classical music.*
- *Read great works of literature.*
- *Memorize where the major countries are.*
- *Learn about guns.*

On Tuesday, I woke up and I immediately started worrying about Ailis and *Battle for Santa Cruz.* Under no circumstances could I let this become a date. I had to make sure the "just friends" part was absolutely clear. I rehearsed a little speech I would give her. How it was great that we were going to the movies and that it was nice to have a friend who was a girl, but who was not a "girlfriend," because there was a big difference.

After breakfast though, I forgot about Ailis and started

thinking about my private-investigator business again. I skateboarded to the Venice library and asked the guy who worked there if they had any books on starting a business. He asked what kind of business, and I said "private investigator" and he looked at me like that was the dumbest thing he'd heard in his life. But he helped me anyway. We found a book that had a couple good tips in it. Like get a separate bank account. And get business cards. But that didn't really explain about being a private investigator. Then he found me a book by a guy who was a bodyguard and personal trainer to the stars. But I would never do that. I was more about finding people. Maybe that would be my catchphrase:

ROBERT CALLAHAN

PRIVATE INVESTIGATOR

"I FIND PEOPLE."

So then I had to get a library card so I could check out *Starting a Small Business*. But I couldn't, because I had no proof that I lived at Hope's. Plus I had no personal ID. I pretended I'd left my wallet at home. The guy could tell I was lying, but then he said "whatever" and made me a card anyway.

On my way out, I saw a rack of classical-music CDs and stopped to look at that. But I didn't really think the classical-music thing was going to work for me. Then, on a different rack of CDs, I saw Mötley Crüe's *Shout at the Devil*, which I hadn't heard since sixth grade. Talk about classical music!

So I grabbed that. I wandered around some more and found a whole section of books about aliens and UFOs, which I stayed to look at. So I ended up at the library pretty much all morning.

When I got home, I still had three hours until *Battle for Santa Cruz*. Since Hope wasn't home, I washed some of my clothes in her washing machine. Not that it was a real date, but somehow I felt like that was the right thing to do. Clean myself up. Act normal. So Ailis wouldn't feel like the only guy who would hang out with her was a dirty street kid.

So then I had clean clothes and I took a shower and even washed my hair and tried to brush it a little bit with one of Hope's brushes. I found a new zit in the mirror and popped it, which turned out to be the wrong call. These British girls I met once told me that in England they call them "spots," and that's pretty much what this one turned into.

When it was time, I skateboarded down the boardwalk toward Santa Monica and the Nuart Theatre. I cruised along, watching the sky turn purple and the ocean become smooth and the tourists take pictures of the setting sun. People never get tired of taking that picture: the sun disappearing into the ocean, the end of the day, the end of their vacation...and then back on the plane to Ohio or Wisconsin or wherever they came from, someplace where they don't have seagulls or palm trees or the sounds of waves crashing in their dreams at night.

FIVE

There was a pretty good crowd at the Nuart, since everyone with half a brain loves a good alien-invasion movie. I kicked up my board and found Ailis waiting in line for tickets. As I walked up, though, I saw two other people I recognized. Right in front of Ailis were the guys who beat the crap out of Chad Mitchell. One of them was wearing Chad's gold watch.

That bugged me.

But I didn't let it affect my non-date with Ailis. "Hey," I said to her.

"Hey," she said, smiling brightly. She was dressed nice, hair clean, cute T-shirt. She even smelled good. Which was bad because it meant she thought this was a date.

I checked the two guys in front of us. They were cleaned

up too: new Nikes, new jeans, probably all of it freshly stolen. Up close, they looked older, in their mid-twenties, probably. They were tall and lanky and had a certain menacing look about them. But they also looked smart and kind of devious, and like they didn't miss much of what happened around them. They looked *evil*, I guess, is the best way to put it. The words *Evil Twins* came into my mind, though they didn't really look alike or appear to be related.

I turned back toward Ailis. She had her big plastic glasses on. "So what's up?" I said. "What did you do today?"

"I go to school, remember?" she answered.

"Of course I remember. What did you do at school?"

She pushed her glasses up her nose. "Well, actually, we had a pretty interesting discussion today in psychology class. About narcissism and how some people are so self-absorbed it affects their entire view of the world."

The Evil Twins, hearing a female voice, turned toward Ailis. "Narcissism?" said the closer one. He had dyed-blond hair. "I've heard of that."

Ailis accepted them into our conversation without thinking. "Lots of people have heard of it. But they don't know what it means. It's not just about looking at yourself in the mirror."

"Which I, personally, *never do*," said the blond Evil Twin, joking around.

"He's lying," said the darker-haired twin. "That's all he does."

"A real narcissist," continued Ailis, "in psychological terms, is a person who can't relate to other people, except as an audience."

"Wow, you're good," the blond twin said. "Where'd you learn that?"

"Santa Monica Community College," said Ailis proudly.

"A college girl," said the dark-haired twin in a flirty way. "I thought you looked smart."

"Smart and cute," said the blond twin.

"Maybe lose the glasses," said the dark-haired twin.

"I kinda like the glasses," said the blond twin.

They both laughed. Ailis even laughed. She was charmed. I couldn't believe it. These criminals, these thugs, were *charming* Ailis.

I couldn't allow this. When the line moved forward, I grabbed Ailis's elbow and pointed her toward a poster on the wall beside us.

"Look," I said. "I've been waiting for that movie."

Unfortunately, the poster was for a movie I'd never heard of called *Love Cats*.

"You have?" said Ailis, staring at me strangely. "Why? It's about a woman and her cats."

I noticed the Evil Twins had turned back around. Mission accomplished.

"Perfect," I said. "I like women. And I like cats."

"But it's a romantic comedy."

"I like romantic comedies," I said.

34

"I don't believe you," said Ailis. "Tell me one romantic comedy you've seen. Ever. In your life."

"I haven't seen that many. But I'm going to start. I need to learn how women think."

"Oh really? And why do you need to do that?"

"Because," I said. "I'm thinking of starting a business."

"What sort of business?"

I didn't want to say. Ailis would probably just laugh. And the Evil Twins were still in hearing distance.

"I haven't decided yet," I said.

We got inside the theater and I steered us far away from the twins. We found seats.

"By the way, I made you a classical CD," Ailis told me. "It's got parts from the most famous symphonies. And I wrote down the names and composers."

"I think I gave up on that," I said, slouching back. "I got a Mötley Crüe CD instead."

"Well, I already finished making it. You can listen to it if you want."

"Okay," I said. "Thanks."

The movie finally started. Thank god. It was about alien spaceships that come to Earth and start blasting away. There'd been a lot of movies like that lately. Personally, this is one of my favorite themes in movies. Aliens attacking. Humans fighting back. I mean, it may not be *War and Peace*, but it's still a classic story, in its own way.

❋ ❋ ❋

After the movie, the Evil Twins were standing against the wall outside the theater. I glanced over at them as we left. I couldn't help myself. The dark-haired twin was still wearing Chad Mitchell's thick gold watch.

They caught me watching them. "Hey," the blond twin said.

I averted my eyes and kept walking. I tried to speed Ailis along.

"Hey!" he said again, more loudly. Ailis, unfortunately, stopped and turned toward them.

"What?" she said.

The blond twin smiled at Ailis. "I was wondering if you want to hang out sometime. Maybe talk some *psychology*..."

Ailis wasn't sure how to respond.

"That your boyfriend?" said the other twin.

"No," she said. "I mean, we're just—"

"*Yes*," I said, gently tugging her away. "I'm her boyfriend."

"I wouldn't be so sure about that," said the blond twin quickly. He took a few steps toward us.

Confused, Ailis turned to me.

"C'mon, let's go," I whispered to her.

"What's the rush?" said the blond twin, coming closer still. "Maybe we need to figure out who the girl wants to be with. Doesn't appear to be you, dude."

I pulled hard on Ailis's arm. This time she came with me.

The twins watched us go.

"That's right, run away!" said the dark-haired twin.

"Dorks in love!" shouted the blond twin as we escaped down the street.

Ailis and I ended up eating fish tacos at a food truck. We sat on the curb in the parking lot and tried not to get fish juice on our clean clothes.

Ailis didn't say anything, and I began to worry about what was said, back at the movie theater.

"Uh," I said. "You know back there . . . with those guys . . . when I said I was your . . ."

"I know you're not my boyfriend," she said. "Duh."

Then I felt worse.

"I mean, it's not that I *couldn't* be your boyfriend. It's just that . . ."

"I know," said Ailis. "You were just trying to protect me."

"Right. Exactly."

"Are you really bored right now?" she asked.

"No."

"Are you having at least a little bit of fun?"

"Yes, of course," I said.

"Then why are you so worried?"

"I'm not worried."

"You seem very worried that I might like you."

"I don't think that," I said, which was not quite true.

"We can just be friends, you know," said Ailis. "We don't even have to decide what we are, if we don't want to."

"That's what I was thinking," I said, holding my fish taco. "But you're a better talker than I am."

"I'm not a better talker. I just know what I'm trying to say."

After that, Ailis and I drove around in her mother's car. We listened to the radio. We talked about the movie more, which was a much easier topic of conversation. We talked about invading alien armies and what sort of resources they might need from our planet. Maybe they would need something simple and obvious, like water or oil. Or maybe they would need something you wouldn't think of, like Styrofoam.

It actually turned into a pretty fun night. When Ailis pulled up at Hope's house, I didn't want to get out. I tried to think of somewhere else we could go, so we could drive around some more.

She saw me hesitating. "Now what's the matter?" said Ailis.

"Nothing," I said.

She stared at me. "I'm not that nerdy, you know," she said. "I'm pretty normal if you get to know me."

"I never said you were nerdy," I said.

"You act like it."

"I don't mean to," I said.

"Thanks for going to the movies."

"Sure. Anytime," I said. I got out of the car.

And then I did something I was totally not planning to

do. I turned back toward her. "You wanna go see that *Love Cats* movie?" I said.

She looked at me. "Do you?"

"Yeah," I heard myself say.

"I don't know if I have time," she said. "But maybe."

I unlocked Hope's front door and went inside. I crept through the living room, trying not to wake up the six animal-rights activists who had come from San Francisco for a big demonstration. One very large woman was snoring loudly on the couch. I let myself out the back door.

In the backyard, the Christmas lights were still on, so I unplugged them, and the backyard went dark and quiet. I liked that, the sudden absence of everything. And then eventually, once your eyes adjusted, you could see the stars.

I climbed into my treehouse and got into my sleeping bag and lay there thinking about my private-investigator business. What would it be like? Where would my office be? What kind of car would I drive? It seemed like a pickup truck would be good. That way you could move stuff around and be a laid-back, workingman's private investigator. Or maybe glamour was the thing. Maybe you needed a Porsche or a Mercedes to impress people. Like if you had to pull up at a casino and adjust your tuxedo or whatever. You couldn't do that in a pickup.

Then I thought about getting off work some night and locking up my private-investigator office and driving home.

I'd pull up into my driveway and open my front door and say, "Honey, I'm home!" My wife would come out of the kitchen and kiss me on the cheek, and I'd ask her what was for dinner.

That was weird, though. Because as I lay there and pictured this, I saw who that woman was. Who my brain had randomly picked out as my someday-in-the-future wife.

It was Ailis.

SIX

A couple days later, another unusual-looking man showed up at the basketball courts. I got an instant feeling about this guy. He was wearing a red track jacket, not like the coat and tie Bruce Edwards had worn. This guy looked like an ex-jock, tanned and leathery.

He stood around and watched our game. When it was over, I sat on the bleachers. He waited until the next game started and made his way over. "You Cali?" he asked.

"Yup," I said, drinking from a water bottle.

"My name is Buckalter," he said. He had a gruff, throaty voice.

"Okay," I said.

He put one foot up on the bottom row of the bleachers.

He crossed his arms over his knee. "I need some help," he said. "I need to find someone."

I took a long drink of my water. I glanced at his face for a minute. Though he looked like a serious person, he also seemed low-key. Like this situation was nothing. It was just a small thing he had to take care of while he dealt with bigger things.

"Who sent you?" I asked.

"A friend of Bruce Edwards's."

"Okay."

"The man I'm looking for. His name is Mugs. He hangs around down here. You know him?"

"Not personally," I said. I'd never spoken to Mugs, but I knew who he was. Everyone did. He was a local bum, a real "character." I hadn't seen him around in a while.

"You think you could look around for me?"

"Sure," I said casually.

"Here's some info on him," said Buckalter, handing me a large manila envelope. "And a little advance money."

I laid the envelope down without opening it.

"There's a cell phone in there. Prepaid. My number's in it. Give me a call if you come up with anything."

I nodded.

"I hear you're a smart kid," said Buckalter, standing up straight again. For some reason, this rubbed me the wrong way. There was no need for the extra flattery. Extra flattery put you in a funny position.

Buckalter watched Diego miss a shot.

"Why are you looking for him?" I said.

"Don't know," he said. "But a guy like that"—he nodded toward the envelope—"could be anything...family...long-lost relatives...Maybe he inherited some money."

"It might help if I knew which it was," I said.

Buckalter frowned. "*You're* looking for him because *I'm* looking for him," he said, still watching the basketball game. "And I'm looking for him because I'm getting paid. Is that gonna be a problem?"

Our eyes met for a moment. "No," I said, thinking that was the professional thing to say.

"Good."

When he was gone, I looked in the envelope. There was a fact sheet, a police file, a couple photos, and a cheap, disposable cell phone.

And quite a bit of money.

That night, I went on Hope's computer and checked Buckalter's info against what I could find out for myself. It all matched up. Mugs's real name was Edwin Torres. He was originally from Phoenix, Arizona. He had been married once, at nineteen. He had been sued several times for child support in his twenties. From thirty on, he lived the life of a homeless person. He had a long police record: vagrancy, assault, public drunkenness, resisting arrest.

The main thing that struck me, he was only thirty-six.

I would have guessed him to be fifty-six from the times I'd seen him on the boardwalk. That was another thing I needed to work on. Knowing how old people were. One time Diego and I got in an argument about how old one of the waitresses was at the Sidewalk Cafe. We started a contest of guessing people's ages. We stopped people on the boardwalk and told them we were doing it as a school project. I was good with the teenagers. I was always within a year or two. But with the older people I was sometimes off by ten years. And the bums were hardest of all. Living all those years outside in the elements, you could miss by fifteen years, easy. I had to practice that more. Maybe there was a book about it at the Venice library.

I went to my treehouse and got out a notebook. What else did I know about Mugs? I'd never talked to him myself. I'd seen him around, standing at the chess tables, talking crap like everybody does. He was one of those guys who always "knew the score." How the world was rigged against the little guy. How the rich could do anything they wanted. When he wasn't talking conspiracies, he wanted you to buy him some wine or give him a ride somewhere or loan him twenty bucks.

I wondered what sort of family situation would make someone come looking for him. Maybe his kid was searching for his long-lost father. If he was, I felt sorry for that kid.

Or maybe some long-lost relative had died and Mugs had

inherited a million dollars. That would be pretty funny. You always heard rumors like that: different street people having secret fortunes. Like Crazy Janet, who hung out at the chess tables. People claimed she had family money stashed away somewhere. Or the old guy who lived beneath the Santa Monica Pier, who was supposedly a famous movie director in the eighties. Or Joey One Shoe, who bummed change on Washington Boulevard; people said he still got royalty checks from some song he wrote thirty years ago. . . .

You'd hear that stuff. And it was fun to think about. But mostly it wasn't true. Most homeless people were just plain messed up. There was no happy ending, no secret bank account. That's why you had to get off the street. Which was why I took the Mugs job. I wasn't kidding about starting my own private-investigator agency. It wasn't some dream. I needed to find something I could do, and do well, and make a business out of it.

If I didn't, who knew where I'd end up.

SEVEN

I began my search for Mugs on Lincoln Boulevard, along a string of liquor stores, where a lot of local bums hung out.

I first went to the Liquor Warehouse, which was a main gathering place. I cruised up on my skateboard and took a seat on the ground next to two hobo traveler types. I played the age-guessing game with them. I guessed their age to be around forty. They were thirty-three and thirty-six.

Then a really old guy came over and wanted us to buy a bottle of Thunderbird with him. I asked him if he'd seen Mugs. He'd never heard of him.

I asked some other people, sometimes asking, sometimes dropping the name into conversation. "If Mugs was here, he'd say..." But no response.

I saw one of the employees standing outside having a

smoke. He had a shaky, alcoholic look to him. "Hey," I called to him. "You seen Mugs around?"

He shook his head.

I stood up and casually ambled over to him. "I hear he's got puppies for sale," I said. "I wanna get one."

The guy laughed. "Mugs selling puppies...?" he said, shaking his head.

So at least he knew him.

"Where's he living nowadays?" I asked.

"No idea," said the guy. "Probably in the gutter somewhere."

"I heard he was down in Hermosa Beach," I tried.

"Hermosa Beach?" said the guy. "Could be. I wouldn't know."

I skated down to the Community Outreach Shelter. I had gone there myself when I first landed in Venice. I sat on the bench outside, watching the cars drive by. Eventually, a guy came over and asked me for a cigarette.

"Mugs has cigarettes," I said. "I think he's inside."

The name did not register with the guy.

I tried that on every person who went in or out. I'd mention Mugs in passing and watch their face for recognition.

Nothing.

I cruised farther down Lincoln Boulevard and found another gang of bums, sitting on the curb outside the 7-Eleven.

I went over to them. "Anybody got forty cents?" I asked, looking through some change in my hand.

Nobody did. "Come on," I said. "I'll give you half my doughnut."

"I don't want no stinkin' doughnut...." said a particularly filthy old bum.

He looked like a guy Mugs might know. "C'mon, forty cents," I pleaded with him.

"Get away from me," he grumbled. "Punk kid."

I looked at him more closely. "I know you! You're friends with Mugs!"

"Mugs," he scoffed, waving his dirty hand. "That bastard!"

"Yeah?" I laughed. "He rip you off?"

"He couldn't rip me off. How you gonna rip me off? What ya gonna take from me?"

I smiled and sat down next to him, then moved away a little because he stank. "Mugs is a true character," I said. "That's for sure."

"Mugs is a punk and a loudmouth," the bum declared. "That's all Mugs is."

"Where'd he go, anyway?" I asked. "I gotta talk to him about a puppy."

"Hell if I know."

"San Diego," I said. "That's what I heard."

"San Diego? Nah! Mugs would never go there. What's in San Diego? Nothing but a bunch of no-good...do-nothing...San Diego? I piss on San Diego!"

"Besides the puppy, Mugs owes me twenty bucks," I said.

"That'll be twenty bucks you never see again!" The bum laughed.

"Where the hell is he anyway?" I said.

"He's probably holed up in Topanga, living in that trailer with his old lady."

That was the thing about crazy old people. If you talked to them long enough, you'd hit these little pockets of sanity. Like inside their jumbled brains were actual facts, actual information. You just had to be willing to wade through the confusion.

"Mugs got an old lady?" I laughed. "No way. That's impossible!"

"Some ol' biker chick. She don't know no better."

"Ha-ha. Well if he's got an old lady, then he must have my money. I think I'll cruise down there. Where was it, exactly?"

"I dunno. Topanga. Down by the beach somewhere."

I thanked him and wandered off, really casual-like. But once I was around the corner, I skated hard toward home. My heart pounded. What if I could find Mugs? I'd be two for two! Three for three if you counted the kid who stole bicycles.

I was totally going to be a private investigator. I was good at this.

I called Ailis and asked her if she felt like driving to Topanga that night. She couldn't; she had a babysitting job.

So I took the bus. It was dark when I got there. The town of Topanga wasn't much, just a couple restaurants along the Pacific Coast Highway. There were two large parking lots below the road, by the beach. One was full of old trailers and hippie vans and broken-down RVs. Drifter-types would camp there for as long as they could before the cops or the sanitation department kicked them out.

I walked along the Pacific Coast Highway and then down the hill to the drifter parking lot. There was an ancient school bus near the entrance that was so packed full of trash and other crap you couldn't see in through the windows. The stuff was piled up right to the ceiling. Old newspapers, rags, appliances, plastic bottles, milk crates. There was even an old washing machine and some other junk tied to the roof.

I circled around it, gawking at the crap. Then I nearly stumbled over its owner in the dark. He was an old guy and he was sitting in a lawn chair facing the ocean. He held a little dog in his lap.

"Oh," I said, bumping him. "Sorry."

He stared up at me, then looked away with a sneer. I guessed his age to be about . . . sixty. But I really had no idea.

"What's up?" I said.

He didn't answer.

"Can I guess your age?" I asked.

He stared at me. "Why would you want to do that?"

"It's for a school project. Let me try."

He turned away, ignoring me.

I studied him in the dim light of the highway above us. He had gray hair, a white beard. "Sixty," I said.

"Nope."

"Sixty-five?"

"Nope."

"Fifty-five?"

"Nope."

"Huh," I said. "Well, how old are you?"

"I don't have to tell you that."

"I know," I said. "But it's for a school project."

He sank into a stubborn silence. That was not a good sign.

"Is Mugs around?" I asked.

"Nope."

"I'm supposed to meet him."

He sneered. The dog also sneered.

"You know where he is?" I asked.

"No idea."

I looked around at the twenty or so other trailers, vans, and RVs scattered around the huge parking lot. "Which one of these is his old lady's?"

"I couldn't tell you that," he said in his difficult way.

I smiled. "Seriously, how old are you? I'm doing a thing for school. I'm supposed to ask twenty people."

"I don't have to tell you nothin'."

"You're sixty-seven."

"Nope."

"Fifty-seven?"

"Nope.

"Fifty-eight."

"Nope."

"Give me a hint: more than sixty or less?"

He stared at me with watery, old-man eyes. "I'm sixty-two."

"Okay, so I was close."

"No, you weren't."

"Yes, I was. I said sixty to start."

"That's not close. That's two years off."

"Two years is pretty close."

"No, it isn't."

"Yes, it is."

"No, it isn't."

"Okay," I finally said. "It isn't."

I continued farther into the parking lot. Fortunately, the couple of trailers I could see were on the far end, away from the old man.

I walked in that direction and wandered among the different campers and trailers Mugs might be in. One had lights on inside. I casually stood outside it until I caught sight of the people inside. They were dudes, young surfer types, probably not friends of Mugs's.

I walked around more. The lights of the cars up on the

Pacific Coast Highway reminded me that I would have to take the bus back to Venice. I wondered when the buses stopped running. Probably pretty early. And it was already nine thirty. I had to watch the time.

I looked into another trailer that had lights on. A woman with white hair was in that one. She was reading something. She was not someone you would describe as a biker chick.

I kept moving. I checked one of the darkened trailers. I tried looking in the window. I couldn't see anything. I walked over to another. Nothing to see there, either. I was getting an anxious feeling now. This was not the best place to be prowling around, looking in people's windows.

A car pulled off the highway above me. There was some honking and a commotion—the car must have been blocking traffic. Someone shouted and a car door slammed shut and the car pulled away, to more honking and tire screeching. I retreated into some low trees beside the parking lot and watched the hill above me.

A lone figure slid down the dirt embankment and came stumbling into the parking lot. He was mumbling loudly to himself. He almost tripped over his own feet.

It was Mugs. I remembered him. He was short, wiry, with a scraggly beard and dirty long hair. He seemed drunk or tired or maybe just worn out from life in general.

I stayed behind my tree.

He made his way to the door of one of the darkened trailers.

He dug some keys out of his pocket. He was wobbling on his feet. He couldn't seem to locate the right key.

Then, strangely, the old guy appeared, from the school bus. He walked slowly and with a limp. He was carrying his little dog. "Mugs," he said.

Mugs, in his haze, turned and looked back at him. "Wha—?"

The old guy limped forward. "Some kid was looking for you."

Mugs turned back to his keys and grumbled to himself. "What kid?" he said. "I don' know no kid."

"I told him you weren't around," said the old guy.

"It ain't no business of yours!" snapped Mugs.

"I'm just telling ya...."

"Well, go tell someone who gives a crap!" he shouted.

"Suit yourself, ya miserable bastard," said the old man. He turned and slowly limped away, holding his little dog.

I stayed behind my tree. I watched Mugs try to unlock his trailer. He tried one key; it didn't work. He tried another; it didn't work, either. He swore and spat on the ground. "Gawddammit!" he said to no one.

Finally he got the door open. He stumbled inside and the door banged shut behind him. A light came on.

From the trees, I could see Mugs staggering around in the trailer.

Why would anybody be looking for him? I wondered. He seemed like such a pathetic creature.

I stayed where I was and waited. I wanted to see if his "old lady" was in there too, or if she would show up. But no one else appeared. I watched for twenty minutes. Mugs lurched around inside the trailer for a bit. Then he disappeared. He must have lay down with the lights still on. Ten more minutes went by. Nothing moved in the trailer.

Now I began to worry about catching the bus home. It was almost eleven. I crept across the parking lot and then silently ran back toward the entrance. The old man had gone inside his school bus.

I ran to the highway and jogged to the bus stop. With six minutes to spare, I caught the last bus back to Venice.

I sat in the back. I took a long breath to calm myself. Then I got out Buckalter's disposable cell phone. As the empty bus shuddered and banged along, I called the one number in the contacts.

"Buckalter," said the voice.

"It's me. Cali."

"Ahh," he said. "Cali the kid."

"I found Mugs."

"Where is he?"

"He's in a trailer in the parking lot below Topanga Canyon. The trailer's a Streamliner. Blue and white. All the way on the right."

"Good job, kid."

"Can I ask one thing, though?"

"Sure," he said.

"What on earth do you want him for?"

"That's none of my business, kid. And it's none of yours, either."

"I just can't imagine—"

"Don't waste your brainpower. You did your job. I'll send you a check. Don't spend it all at once."

EIGHT

The check came two days later. It was big. Really big. So big that I couldn't sign it over to Hope. I had to go to the bank myself. Even then the bank lady had to call Hope's friend who worked at a different bank to confirm I wasn't a drug dealer or some other criminal.

So then I had all this money. The first thing I thought was to buy an old car, but I couldn't do that, because I was still technically—legally—a ward of the state of Nebraska. And not in good standing, since I'd run away. Not that anyone was actually looking for me, three years later. But if I tried to get a driver's license, my status would show up in the computers and then there'd be trouble. So no car. Not for now, anyway.

So I bought some other stuff: Hope's old laptop, so I

wouldn't have to be on her computer all the time; matching yellow watches for Diego's sisters Pilar and Izzy, who left me free bags of oranges on Fridays. I also got a new wet suit since the one I found in the alley smelled bad, which was probably why it was in the alley in the first place.

Then I decided to take Ailis to dinner and the movies. I'd actually been avoiding her since we never went to *Love Cats*. But when it came right down to it, she was my only friend who was my age, and seminormal, and didn't live out of a shopping cart or whatever.

So we drove to this fancy sushi place. It was awkward and we didn't know what to order. Or how to use chopsticks. I ended up with some little rings that were octopus tentacles or something. Ailis got this sticky lump of fish that looked like somebody's finger.

When we got to the movies, I bought us a bunch of candy and two huge tubs of popcorn, which we chomped down on top of our weird fish dinner. Which wasn't a good idea.

"Where did you get all that money?" Ailis asked me afterward, sitting in her car, both of us feeling woozy and nauseous. She had seen how my wallet was stuffed with twenties.

"I helped this guy," I said, avoiding the subject and rolling down the window in case I puked.

She didn't seem impressed—more like suspicious. And annoyed with me in general. It was the opposite of what I thought would happen. I always thought people liked you more if you had some cash to throw around. But it didn't seem to be the case with Ailis. The whole night was pretty much a disaster.

But I still had all this money. Diego and I were hanging out at the chess tables, and I asked him what present he would buy someone if he could get anything, for anyone.

"I'd buy Jojo some basketball shoes," he said. "Some super nice ones."

It was true. Jojo mostly wore shoes he found around the boardwalk or in the trash. He deserved better. And think how much better he'd play.

So the two of us got on our skateboards and headed to the big Nike store in Santa Monica.

I'd never actually been in that store. It was super slick, with huge video screens and music playing and different artificial surfaces to test your shoes on. We found a salesman and I told him about Jojo, his height, his weight, his explosiveness, how he could dunk on dudes a foot taller than him.

The salesman just stared at us.

Then we noticed two security guards behind us, one of them talking into a walkie-talkie. We were like, "What did we do?"

They thought we were shoplifters. Or street people. Or something bad. I guess we looked a little rough around the edges. Not like the other shoppers who were all super neat and clean and wore brand-new Nike stuff, head to foot.

"Never mind them," said Diego. We went into the

basketball section and figured it out for ourselves. We got the brand-new Air Jordans, with reinforced arch support, soft leather interior, and shiny red outer shell. I paid for them on the spot: $239 cash. The sales guy didn't mind us so much then.

We were psyched! When we got back to Venice, we told everyone to come to the basketball courts the next day, at noon, for the presenting of the Air Jordans to Jojo. It would be a big event, a big surprise.

The next day, everyone was there, gathered around the main court. Jojo's team had just won their third game in a row. That was when I stepped down out of the bleachers and announced in my loudest voice, "Jojo, today you're gonna get something for your efforts!" Everyone started gathering around and clapping in rhythm. Jojo didn't understand at first. Then Diego walked out with the Nike bag and lifted it up high so everyone could see. People went nuts, yelling and clapping and cheering for our man! Naturally, Jojo teared up. He always cries whenever anyone acknowledges him, or claps for him, or shows him love in any way.

But he still didn't understand what was happening. Finally, he got it: The Nike bag was for him. Diego handed it over. Jojo opened it, looked inside, pulled out the shoe box. He laid it on the ground and about a hundred people bent down to watch. "Open it, Jojo!" people said.

He did. He opened the box and there they were. The amazing shoes!

At first, he didn't understand. He seemed happy to see them, but he didn't know what they were for. Finally someone shouted, "They're for you, Jojo!"

"They're a present!" Diego said.

Slowly, he began to understand.

"They're from all of us!" I said, gesturing to everyone.

"We love you, Jojo!" someone yelled out.

"We love playin' ball with you, brother!" said someone else.

"You're the best in the world!" yelled a third person.

When he realized what was happening, he put them on, with no socks, of course, since he didn't have any. Everyone cheered and clapped and whistled some more. Then everyone backed away and he did a couple spectacular dunks so everyone could see the bright red shoes in action. It was like a big party, everyone laughing and joking and admiring Jojo's new shoes, which looked amazing.

I thought it went great. I was so happy. Diego and I high-fived. Just like Hope and other people had helped me out, now I'd done the same for Jojo.

Later that afternoon, Diego and I were down at the chess tables, drinking Mountain Dew with Tommy Shirts and a bunch of other guys. We were laughing and talking and telling people about our present. Tommy Shirts was deeply impressed with our generosity and thought maybe he should get a present too. In fact, whatever direction the conversation went, he steered it right back to things he needed, and what would be a good present for him. In case anyone wanted to give him one.

Then a guy rode by on a skateboard. He had the same Air Jordans we gave to Jojo. Diego pointed them out to the other guys. "See those?" he said. "Those are just like the shoes we gave Jojo. Just like that."

Everyone admired the shoes. Everyone said we had good taste. There was some more high-fiving. But then the guy wearing the shoes glanced back at us. He had an odd, slightly guilty expression on his face.

He sped up.

"What the...?" I said out loud.

"Oh no..." said Diego.

We both jumped to our feet and took off running after the guy. But he saw us coming and sped up even more. We had no chance.

We gave up and then hurried down the boardwalk in the other direction. We found Jojo, who was taking a nap in his little cardboard shack behind the tattoo parlor. We yanked back the old blanket and found him asleep on his dirty yoga mats. On his feet were a pair of horrible Kmart sneakers. They had a picture of SpongeBob on the sides of them. We shook him awake and we were like, "Jojo! Some skater dude stole your shoes!"

He was like, "No, no, no..."

We were like, "Yes! We just saw him!"

But Jojo was like, "No, no. He didn't steal them. I gave them to him. He needed them. So we traded."

Diego and I looked at the SpongeBob shoes. We looked at Jojo. We looked at each other. Of course Jojo gave them away. He gave everything away.

Poor Jojo started to apologize, but we were like, it's all right, it's not your fault, we understand. And then Diego felt bad because it was his idea to get them in the first place. But I told him it was okay, it was nobody's fault. We tried. That was all that mattered.

I did one other stupid thing with my money. I got talked into paying for a little birthday party Tommy Shirts and some of the guys were throwing for Grumpy George, an older local guy who had no teeth. This meant—at first—paying for a case of beer and some chips, which turned into several cases of beer and some chips and some wine, which turned into all those things plus four large bottles of vodka and a huge order from a local Mexican restaurant since Mexican food was all Grumpy George could eat. Pretty soon I'd given Tommy and the guys about four hundred dollars. Then, before the party even started, Tommy and his buddies decided to stash some of the vodka for later. That started an argument. Which then turned into an actual fight. Which traveled from the chess tables to the alley to the Sidewalk Cafe, like a fight will do. Several tourists ended up covered in black-bean soup. So then the cops came and arrested everyone and took all the alcohol.

In the end, Diego and I had to hide in the storm drain and we didn't even do anything.

As soon as I got back in my treehouse that night, I resolved to keep my money and my private-investigator business to myself. Which was a good idea anyway. Asking questions about people, digging into their lives—that wasn't cool with certain people around the boardwalk, even if it was for a good cause, even if you were helping Mugs get reunited with his family or whatever.

If that's even what happened.

So that's what I did. I hung out, I played basketball, I surfed. I listened to Mötley Crüe. I checked out a book called *The Big Sleep*, which the guy at the library said I should read since it was about a private detective.

And then Ailis showed up again. She came out to the treehouse one night after eating dinner with Hope and some of her woman friends. This was a couple of weeks after our disastrous sushi/movie night. Things had gone back to normal between us. An awkward acquaintanceship. We hadn't gone to any other movies. We hadn't really spoken.

"Cali?" she said.

"Hi, Ailis," I said, pushing open my little door and looking down. She stood barefoot in the yard. Hope was making everyone take off their shoes lately, because that's what people did in Japan.

"I saw a brochure at the community college and I thought

64

you might be interested in it." She held it up in the air, as if I could read it from there.

"What's it for?"

"It's about getting your GED."

"What's that?"

"It's a test you take. And if you pass, you get a high school diploma."

I had vaguely heard of this.

"There's a whole program for it," she said. "You take some classes and then you take the test. It's pretty easy. Maybe you should do it."

This was the hard part about Ailis. It was easy to think of her as an annoying person. But then she would do these little things for you. Like making the classical-music CD. Or now this. She was, in her robotic way, looking out for me.

"Okay," I said, staring down at her. "I'll take a look."

"Do you want it now?" she said.

"Yeah, sure."

"Do you want me to leave it inside?"

"Okay," I said. I watched her standing in the grass in her bare feet. It was a nice night. The outside lights were on, so the whole backyard looked like a movie set.

"Or do you want me to come up?" she said.

Oh great, I thought. Ailis wanted to see inside the tree-house. I knew that would happen. No matter if you're seven or seventeen, if you have a fort, a girl wants to come in it.

"You want to come up here?" I asked.

"I mean, it would be better than leaving it in the house, don't you think?"

I didn't, but whatever.

"Well, I don't mind if you come up. But you gotta climb the ladder. It isn't easy."

"I know how to climb a ladder," she said.

She went to the wooden ladder, gripped it, tried the first step with her bare foot. It wasn't super graceful, but she did it. She climbed up.

I had to move away from the door to let her in. It wasn't a big treehouse. Maybe ten feet by eight feet. I had the light on and the radio was playing softly. There were some notebooks scattered around and *The Big Sleep* and the front half of *War and Peace.*

Ailis crawled in on all fours. I had backed up and was sitting against the wall.

Ailis looked around. "Wow," she said.

I have to say, not to brag or anything, but the inside of my treehouse is pretty sweet. The outside, I'd left looking half-assed and randomly nailed together, so people wouldn't break in. But the inside had carpet and a lightbulb and two little shelves for my clothes and stuff. It was all waterproofed and there was a little hatch in the ceiling you could open if you wanted to look at the sky before you fell asleep. The only bad thing was the low ceiling. You couldn't stand all the way up. You did most of your moving around on your hands and knees.

Still, Ailis was impressed. "What's that?" she asked, pointing to the hatch.

"That's the roof," I said.

"What's up there?"

"The rest of the tree," I said.

Ailis saw the little hot plate I'd brought up recently. I'd intended to make hot chocolate at night, but it was too much trouble to bring water up and mix it and clean your cup and all that. So I just did it inside.

"Can we go up there?" said Ailis, pointing back to the hatch.

"Sure."

We crawled onto the roof. Now I was actually worried for Ailis because you could fall off the roof. There were no walls, no railings. And it was high up. So I made her sit in the middle.

"I'm not gonna fall," she said.

"I know. But the view's better in the middle."

So then we both lay on our backs on the roof and stared into the sky. The tree swayed slightly and the moon was out and you could smell the ocean and hear the waves in the distance. It was pretty fun, having another person there. Even if it was just Ailis.

NINE

There's one thing about living in a tree: You notice the weather.

I woke up early the next morning and I knew instantly something was up. I could smell it in the air. I could feel it in the motion of the tree.

A big storm was rolling in off the Pacific. I got dressed and climbed down into the grass. I cruised on my skateboard to the boardwalk. Huge dark clouds were moving in off the ocean like monstrous alien ships. The wind blew. The ocean was wound up and crashing around. Not big clean waves, like you might surf on, but lots of little ones, all jittery and churning and bouncing into each other. The seagulls hunkered down in the wind and crows leaped around on the boardwalk, squawking and fighting over pizza scraps and french fries and being pretty bold about it, since the humans had cleared out.

I went over to the Pizza Slice and got a slice and ended up talking to a girl sitting on the curb outside. Her name was Strawberry and she had run away from somewhere back east. She didn't look so good. She'd slept in the alley the night before, like right on the ground.

I found myself advising her. I don't usually tell people what to do, but for some reason I couldn't help myself. I told her she needed to get a deal like I got. Find someone to take you in. Live in someone's garage or something. Pay a little rent if you had to, just don't sleep outside. Things can get rough on the boardwalk at night. You need to be somewhere with a roof over your head. Not sleeping on the ground in the alley.

She didn't really listen, though. She said she liked sleeping outside. She'd done it in Maryland, New Orleans, Tucson. Why couldn't she do it here? The Pizza Slice guy had offered her free pizza to stand on the boardwalk with the PIZZA SLICE $1.99 sign, which she seemed to think was a good deal. She was a little slow, I noticed. I wondered if she was on drugs. I hoped she would be okay. I didn't know that she would.

So then I cruised on my skateboard toward the Milk Bar Cafe on Washington Boulevard. The boardwalk was almost deserted now. Some fat drops of rain had begun to fall. Most of the vendor stalls were closed or closing.

I coasted past a guy leaning on his car. He'd driven right up onto the walkway, where you weren't normally allowed to drive. He watched me pass. He studied my face, my board.

"Hey!" he yelled after me. "You know a guy named Cali?"

I swung my board around and stopped.

"I might," I said.

He came right over to me. "You're him, right?"

I nodded that I was.

"You got a minute?" he said. "I'd like to talk to you. It's important."

We went to Café Italia on Pacific Avenue. He bought me a chai latte and a bagel, and we settled at a table by the window. It was nice to be inside a real café with the storm outside. It was cozy.

The guy's name was Grisham. He was a private investigator. He showed me his ID. It was in a leather holder that you could flip open, like on TV.

Unlike the other guys, he didn't tell me what he wanted right off. He seemed not in a hurry. He took care of the little things first. Like putting sugar in his coffee. And stirring it. He had a wide face and a short, military-style haircut. There was a big ring on one of his fingers. It looked like a class ring, or maybe it was something about sports. He looked like he could have played football.

"I was told you know this area," he said to me.

"I hang out a lot," I said.

He smiled. "That's a good strategy. Learn a place. Make it your own. Make it so that if anyone wants to know what's going on, they gotta come to you."

I smiled at the compliment. I drank my chai. I felt comfortable with Grisham. I felt pretty confident in general. I'd found Chad Mitchell and Mugs and the bike stealer. I was three for three.

"Can I ask you something?" I said.

"Of course."

"How'd you get started in the investigator business?"

"Good question," he said, looking out the window. "I started off working with an older guy, an ex-cop. I worked in his office, did the grunt work. Eventually, he let me do some real stuff. When he retired, I took over his clients. And built it up from there."

I nodded.

"I'd offer you a job, but I'm a little far from home on this one. I work out of San Francisco."

I nodded more.

"Anyway," he said. He took a folder out of his briefcase. "I'm looking for a girl. Maybe you can help."

He opened the folder and pulled out a picture of a pretty teenager, about sixteen. The photo was of her and a friend standing on a soccer field. They wore soccer shirts, their hair was braided in an athletic style.

He passed it to me.

"Her name is Reese Abernathy. She's from Palo Alto, California. She ran away from home. We think she's down here somewhere. LA, possibly San Diego."

He handed me some cell phone records.

"Why'd she run away?" I asked.

"Family issues."

He handed me a credit card statement, a police report, a missing-person file. There was also a seven-page statement from her father, detailing the family history, the present situation, how Reese had changed after her mother's death. I skimmed the first couple pages as best as I could.

"How did her mother die?" I asked.

"Suicide," said Grisham.

I flipped through more pages of the statement. "And this happened in San Francisco?"

"Palo Alto. Otherwise known as Silicon Valley. The dad's a big finance guy. Apple, Google, Facebook, he kinda works behind the scenes. Very wealthy. A major player."

He handed me another picture. "Here's a more recent photo."

In this picture Reese looked totally different. No braids, no smiling jock face. She had shoulder-length black hair, dyed. She wore dark lipstick and black mascara. She looked like she'd walked out of a Goth club.

"And here's another," he said. "This one might be the best to see what she actually looks like."

He slid across the table a mug shot. Underneath the plain,

pale, and possibly intoxicated face of Reese Abernathy, it said: SAN FRANCISCO POLICE DEPT. #8726354.

"What's this for?" I asked.

"Shoplifting. Possession of fake ID."

I nodded. I went back to "Jock Reese" and looked at her. I went to "Goth Reese," looked at her. I picked up "Fake ID Reese" and looked at her.

"She likes to change her style," I said.

"I guess so," said Grisham.

"What does it mean when people change their appearance a lot?" I asked.

"That, I wouldn't know," said Grisham. "Why do people dress up like vampires and put rings in their noses?" he said, grunting with disgust. "I don't know that, either."

That seemed a little uncalled for. Reese didn't look like a vampire, or have a ring in her nose. She just dyed her hair and put on some lipstick. And to be honest, that was her best look. "Goth Reese" had some personality. A lot more than "Jock Reese." But a guy like Grisham wasn't going to understand that.

"Does she have a car?" I asked.

"Not that we know of...She's got a California driver's license, though." He found a scanned picture of it and handed it to me. As he did, I saw a black strap under his suit coat. Grisham was carrying a gun, in a concealed shoulder holster. This lent a certain weight to the situation.

He sat back. He looked at me. "So what do you think?" he said.

I shrugged. "I can keep my eyes open. I can't guarantee anything."

"Of course not," said Grisham. "What's your day rate?"

My day rate? I hadn't thought of that. I quickly calculated how much I'd gotten paid per day for the Mugs job. When I came up with a number, I doubled it.

Then I doubled it again.

I said that number to Grisham, who thought about it for about two seconds. "Done," he said.

I tried to not look shocked. I immediately went back to studying the Reese pictures.

"So why exactly did she run away?" I asked.

"It's all in her father's report," he said.

"But in your own mind," I said. "What do you think?"

"In my own mind?" he said, amused. "I have no idea. She's sixteen. Her dad's a high-powered money guy. And her mom just killed herself."

"Why did her mom kill herself?"

Grisham shrugged. "According to the file, she was depressed. Emotional issues. But that's not our problem. Mr. Abernathy is desperate to find his daughter. So that's what we gotta do."

"All right," I said, staring at the various versions of Reese Abernathy. "I'll do what I can. But someone like this, the beach might not be their first option."

"We know that. We're covering everything. This is a big job. There are a lot of people involved. You cover your turf. That's all I ask."

TEN

When Grisham was gone, I felt strange and restless, like the weather, which had gotten worse. I got on my skateboard, held open my coat, and let the wind push me slowly down the boardwalk. It was completely shuttered up now against the rain and the gusting winds. Still, a few brave tourists were out, taking pictures of the storm, I guess. Tommy Shirts was camped in a doorway with some of his buddies, drinking cheap wine. I looked for the new girl, Strawberry, but I didn't see her. Hopefully she'd found some shelter.

I caught the bus to Malibu. Watching out the window, I let my mind rest on the concept of "Reese Abernathy." *Where would she be?* That was the interesting thing about this one. A pretty girl…a *rich* girl…in Los Angeles…no car…alone. Not that she would be alone for long. A girl like that would meet a lot of people very fast. And not in a good way.

Or maybe she was smarter than that. Maybe she had a plan. She had figured out how to get a fake ID. And she wasn't afraid to shoplift. So she wasn't some innocent school-girl type. It was hard to tell. I hadn't known that many rich people in my life. I mean, I *saw* rich people. I saw them every day. But to understand a rich person, a *really* rich person, I wasn't sure I could do that.

I got off the bus in Malibu and skated through the rain to the Starbucks. I got a coffee and found a table while the storm raged outside. I carefully took out the Reese file.

I looked again at the pictures. Soccer Reese looked happy. She had a kind of smirky confidence about her. Goth Reese looked like she was thinking about something. Fake ID Reese, the mug shot—that was harder to read. She looked a little blank in that one, a little lost.

I read through the various papers. The missing-person's police report. A grief counselor's evaluation. There was a note from Reese's sixth-grade art teacher from a place called the Corning School. It said how Reese was an extraordi-narily talented and creative art student. There was even a photograph of a strange gooey painting to illustrate Reese's brilliance.

Then I got to Mr. Abernathy's seven-page essay about his daughter. This I read carefully. Reese was an only child...a good kid...sports...good grades...

Then marital problems...dad working all the time... mother suffers from depression...different treatments... but the Abernathys always do the right thing for their precious daughter....

Then the mother's suicide nine months ago...Reese grows listless, uncommunicative, distraught...she begins hanging around with the wrong people, not coming home on time, risky behaviors...Mr. Abernathy sends her to different doctors, therapists...no one knows what to do....

Near the end, the dad suggested that Reese might be suicidal herself. To one counselor, Reese said that her mother was now "free" and in a place of "no pain." This section of the report was underlined and highlighted. It was considered extra important, a warning.

I drank my coffee. I sorted through the various printouts. Unlike Chad Mitchell, Reese did not leave a trail with a credit card. Either she didn't have one, or she wasn't using it. Which was smart on her part. But that meant she had cash. Or could get cash when she needed it.

Eventually, I gathered the papers and put them back in the folder. Then I sipped the last dregs of my coffee and stared out the window.

Reese Abernathy. Where would a person like that go? What would they do?

I had no idea.

ELEVEN

On Tuesday, I had my first GED class. Ailis was excited I was going. She wanted to pick me up, since she had a class that night too. So we rode there together.

I found the GED orientation room. It was a mix of foreigners and assorted hard-luck types: high school dropouts, stoned skateboarders, people who looked like they'd been in jail.

We sat in rows of chairs. They gave us a book and we went around the room reading out loud. Then they divided us up. They put me in with the slightly smarter people, which wasn't saying much. One of the guys in my group was a wiry, intense guy I'd seen on the boardwalk. He was a brawler type, his head was shaved, and you could tell by the multiple scars on his skull that he'd had his head cracked a few times.

I gave him a little nod of recognition, which he returned. When the teacher read our names, he answered to Jackson Moretti, but he told her that everyone called him "Jax." When she called my name, Robert Callahan, I told her everyone called me "Cali." But the teacher wasn't impressed with our nicknames. She would call us "Jackson" and "Robert" in the classroom.

When class was over, Ailis was standing by the vending machines, waiting for me. I was pretty drained by then. It was pretty stressful reading out loud and being called "Robert" for two hours.

"But you did it," she said. "You finished your first day!"

"Yeah," I said. "I guess I did."

It was only eight thirty, so Ailis and I went to the burger place across the street. We got some fries and two milk shakes.

"So what did you think of college?" she asked me.

"Not really my thing," I said honestly.

"You just think that because you've never been to school before."

"I've been to school."

"I bet you'll like it," she said. "If you give it a chance. You tried classical music."

"What I really need is a business class."

"Oh really?" she said. "And what sort of business are you planning to go into?"

I'd avoided telling Ailis about my career plans, but now

that I was looking for Reese Abernathy, I felt more confident. I was really doing it. I was getting paid.

"I'm going to be a private investigator," I said.

Ailis nearly spit out her milk shake. "A *private investigator*?" She laughed.

"I'm serious."

"I'm sure you are," Ailis said, grinning. "Or maybe you could be an astronaut? Or a fireman? Or maybe you could be president of the United States?" She smiled at her own jokes.

"Actually," I said into my own milk shake, "I'm already doing it. That's how I got that money."

Ailis laughed some more. Then she stopped. "Wait, the money from the sushi restaurant?"

"Yes," I said.

"All those twenties? You got that being a private investigator?"

"Yes," I said quietly. "I mean, I don't have a license or anything. I'm more of a freelancer."

She looked at me a long time. She seemed to almost believe me. "What do you do exactly?" she asked.

"I look for people."

"What kind of people?"

"Young people mostly. That seems to be my specialty."

She still didn't believe me. She studied my face. "Are you looking for anyone now?"

I had made copies of the pictures of Reese Abernathy. I

got one of them out of my back pocket. I handed it to Ailis. "I'm looking for her."

Ailis unfolded the paper. She studied preppy soccer Reese.

"Her name is Reese Abernathy," I said.

"What did she do?"

"She ran away."

"Like you," said Ailis, looking at the picture.

"That's right."

"Have you ever found anyone?"

"I'm three for three, actually."

"No way," she said.

"I got lucky on the others. This one won't be so easy."

"And someone paid you?"

I nodded.

Ailis handed the picture back to me. She still didn't quite believe me. "Well good for you. I guess."

Ailis was interested, though. You could tell. Back in her car, we drove toward Santa Monica. She began to ask me questions about my other cases and I answered as best I could, without getting too specific. She was still making fun of me, in a way. But she was also genuinely curious. And impressed.

"So like, where do you start?" she asked.

"No place really. I just hang out. And cruise around. And watch people. I've always watched people. Like see those kids," I said, pointing to a gang of street kids with sleeping bags and dreadlocks. "Those guys have been around for a month or so. They live on the beach. They move back and forth between Venice and Santa Monica. They panhandle."

Ailis nodded.

"And that guy," I said, pointing to a sketchy-looking guy checking his phone. "That's Smokin' Joe. He sells weed."

"How about them?" asked Ailis, pointing out three ordinary people talking on the corner.

"Don't know. They look like tourists. Probably foreign."

"How can you tell they're foreign?"

"The hair. The pants. And look at the guy's face. He's not American."

"No way," said Ailis. "You can't tell that from a guy's face."

"Sure you can," I said.

"Americans don't look different than other people," insisted Ailis. "We're all from somewhere else."

"Yeah, but we're heavier, and more bland. Look how chiseled that guy's features are."

"No way."

"Pull over next to him," I said.

She did.

I rolled down my window. I called to the man, "Hey, do know the way to the beach?"

"No," said the man. "It is this way, I think. But I do not know. I am tourist."

"Me too," I lied. "Where you from?"

"Austria," he said.

"Austria," I said. "Thanks."

We pulled away. I rolled up my window. "See?" I said.

"Huh," said Ailis, glancing over at me suspiciously.

We drove around more. I told her the story of Reese's family, her rich dad, her dead mother.

"The real question is," I said, "where would Reese Abernathy go if she were in the area?"

"If she's that rich," said Ailis, "she's not going to be sleeping in her car."

"But where would she go instead?" I asked.

"A hotel maybe?"

"You have to have an ID at a hotel. And a credit card. Even a crappy one."

"What about a youth hostel?"

I hadn't thought of that. I'd heard about youth hostels. They were like group hotels for young travelers. But was there one here in Santa Monica?

Ailis checked her phone. There were three. One of them was a block away.

I'd never been inside a youth hostel before. It was a pretty nice setup. Thirty bucks to sleep in a bunk bed with a bunch of tourist kids from foreign countries. There was a lobby, with a TV and some couches. Young people came and went. Most of them were in their late teens or twenties. I wanted to go inside, but you had to pay for a bed, so I did. I paid for a bed for Ailis too, and gave her the pictures of Reese Abernathy. "Go look around," I told her. "See what you can find."

I went into the boys' area. Some of the guys were already in their bunks, reading, or looking at maps, or planning the next day's sightseeing trips. I talked to them. Where were they from? What were they doing? What did they like about LA? Some of them were helpful. Some could barely speak English. They all had new clothes, though. And nice packs and stuff. Just like Reese would probably have.

I went into the main lounge area and sat with Ailis, who had circulated through the different girls' rooms.

"You see anything?"

"A lot of girls in expensive underwear," said Ailis. "No Reese, though."

We watched the soccer game that was playing on a special European TV network. "I like this place," I said. "I feel like I'm in a foreign country."

I decided to spend the night there, since I'd already paid for a bed. Ailis had to go home.

I walked her back to her car. "Sorry I didn't believe you at first," she said. "About the private-investigator thing."

"That's okay."

"If you need any more help..."

"I might. I might need a car."

"Okay," she said. "Just call me."

"I will. Thanks."

The next morning, when I opened my eyes, I couldn't remember where I was. It reminded me of my first weeks in California. I'd wake up in some cement pipe or under a bridge somewhere, and I'd be like, *Where the hell am I?* That's why I came to Southern California in the first place. So no matter what else happened, I knew I would never freeze to death.

I wasn't freezing now, that's for sure. I was lying in a crisp, clean bunk bed in an international youth hostel. I got out of bed and followed the other guys to the cafeteria. There, I helped myself to a huge plate of waffles and eggs. Sitting with the well-groomed foreign kids, I realized people were staring at me. I kinda stood out. I looked too "surf bum," or just too "bum" in general. I needed a haircut. And more normal clothes. If I was going to be a real investigator, I couldn't look like I lived in a treehouse.

That was three more things for my list:

- *Learn about clothes.*
- *Dress better.*
- *Get a real haircut, like from a barber.*

After breakfast, I sat on the bench outside the youth hostel and watched the people going in and out. I could totally see Reese staying in a place like this. This was a good idea by Ailis, one I never would have thought of.

Then I rode my skateboard to the youth hostel a couple

blocks away. I went in and sat in the lobby. I found a map of Santa Monica and pretended to study it. Two girls came out of the dorm area. They were dressed like Goth Reese, so I listened to them as they studied the big map on the wall and discussed their day's activities.

I walked over to them. "What are you guys doing today?" I asked. I had heard other youth hostel people ask each other this.

"First, we go shop-eeng," said the one girl. They were from France, it turned out. "There eez a Buffalo Exchange down the street."

"Shopping? That's what you do when you travel to another country?"

"Of course. We are girls." They made weird pouting expressions.

"What do you do at night?" I asked them.

"I do not know. Our guidebook mentions zis place Torch-light? Do you know it?"

"Yeah, it's down on Main Street."

"We can go there? Even if we are not twenty-one?"

"Yeah. It's for underage kids. There's music. I could meet you there later if you want."

The girls looked at each other. They shrugged. "Oh-kay," they said.

After that I went to the last youth hostel. This one was the farthest from the beach and the cheapest. The crowd was more diverse in age and more American. There were more tattoos, piercings, etc. A scruffy kid who looked like me came out, with a skateboard and earbuds in. He took off down the sidewalk.

I stood around for twenty minutes, but no Reese. At least I was getting some ideas about where she might be. I went back to downtown Santa Monica and found the Buffalo Exchange store. Sure enough, there were tons of girls there. And the right age too. And the right look. I tried asking one of the counter girls if she'd seen my girlfriend, showing her a picture of Reese. She hadn't.

I was coasting on my skateboard back to Venice when my phone rang. It was Grisham.

"Good news," he said. "She's near you. She used her credit card last night in Hollywood."

"Where did she use it?"

"Some place called the Buffalo Exchange. What is that?"

"It's a used-clothing store," I said.

"Good to know," he said. "And here's the best part: This morning she rented a bike in Venice Beach."

My pulse quickened. "Okay," I said.

"The ball's in your court, kid," he said. "Be a hero. Find the girl."

TWELVE

I got back to Venice as fast as I could. Then I cruised on my skateboard, right down the middle of the boardwalk, scanning the crowds and the bike path for a glimpse of Reese Abernathy. I tried to empty my mind and feel the flow of the tourists as they moved around me. What kind of vibe would Reese give off? And which Reese would she be: Goth Reese? Jock Reese? Something new: Bikini Ray-Bans Reese?

But several trips up and down the boardwalk revealed nothing. If she'd been here, she was not here now.

After a couple hours, I gave up and found Diego at the basketball court. We went to the Pizza Slice. Strawberry, the new girl, was sitting on the curb outside. That had become her spot. She'd been there every day that week. She wasn't looking too good.

Diego and I got slices and sat with her.

"Where you sleepin'?" I asked Strawberry.

"Over there," she said, vaguely waving toward the alley.

"Inside?"

"Yeah."

She was lying. From the look of her, she'd slept under a car. Or in a Dumpster. She had actual trash in her hair. She was dirty and pale. But I didn't say anything.

"You can take showers down where the surfers are," I said, pointing at some guys in wet suits at the outdoor showers.

"In public?"

"Sure. You wear a bathing suit. You got a bathing suit?"

"No," she said.

"You came to California and you don't have a bathing suit?" I said. I reached for my wallet and pulled out a twenty-dollar bill. I stuffed it into the pocket of her hoodie. "Go get a bathing suit."

She didn't seem to hear me.

"Like those guys," I said, pointing to some little kids who were goofing around in the shower with the surfers.

She stared at the kids but did not speak.

I got another slice and went with Diego to the chess tables. It was getting late now, and the sun was going down. I was pretty sure I'd missed Reese. Still, I kept my eye on the board-walk and the bike path.

Diego ate his pizza. I ate mine.

I remembered the tourist guy from Austria. I wasn't sure where that was.

"You know where Austria is?" I asked Diego.

"Isn't that in Texas?"

"No," I said. "I think it's a country."

Diego thought for a moment. "Is it where the kangaroos are?"

"No, that's Africa," I said. But I wasn't sure. I really needed to learn more about other countries. Especially living in Venice, which had tourists from every corner of the earth.

Diego drank from his can of grape soda. I took a bite of pizza and got stuck on one end of a long cheese strand. Diego tried to help by swatting at the strand, but I pushed his hand away. I had my own technique for dealing with cheese strands. I liked to eat my way back to the pizza. I held the slice high up in the air, tilted my head back, and lowered the cheese strand down into my mouth, chewing as I went.

And that's when Reese Abernathy rode by.

She was on a bike. She rode past us, not fast, but not slow either. Just cruising along, like people do.

I nearly fell off the bench when I saw her. I got cheese strand all over my face and shirt. Plus the pizza grease dripped onto my arm. I finally threw the whole mess onto the ground and took off running.

"Cali?" said Diego, having no idea what I was doing.

I ran, pulling the pizza cheese off me. I ran at full speed but she was riding fast and in a few seconds I'd lost her on the crowded boardwalk.

But I kept running. The boardwalk only went another half mile to the south. She'd have to stop or at least slow down when she got to the end of it.

I ran hard. I was flying: through people, around people, dashing and darting between packs of meandering tourists.

I reached the end of the boardwalk and stood in the parking lot at the Venice Pier. Here there were two choices: She'd either turned right and was on the pier, or she'd gone left onto Washington Boulevard. I tried Washington first, jogging quickly up one side of the street and down the other. I checked the bike racks, Dave's Surf Shack, the Milk Bar Cafe....

Nothing. No Reese.

So I ran for the pier.

Now though, I adopted a "jogging" persona, to not call so much attention to myself. I "jogged" onto the pier. It was long, a couple hundred yards or so. You couldn't really see the people at the other end.

When I'd gone halfway, I thought I could make out a girl on a bike, stopped at the far end, gazing into the ocean. It could have been Reese. But I couldn't be sure.

What should I do? Should I call Grisham now? I checked

my pockets and realized *I didn't have my phone.* I had left it in Diego's bag, at the chess tables.

This was a terrible mistake. But I kept moving. I slowed to a fast walk. I watched the people fishing off the railings. Mexican music played on boom boxes. Tourists took pictures of a guy who'd caught a stingray and was reeling it up.

I stayed focused on the lone bike rider. But then the worst possible thing happened. The bike rider turned and started pedaling back toward me. *Crap.* Now what did I do? Try to stop her? Try to talk to her?

I shouldn't have come out here at all, I realized. *I should have waited on the other end!*

I turned then, and started running the other direction. Maybe I could catch her on Washington. Or maybe I could say something as she passed, or stop her, maybe ask directions.

I ran, still being "the jogger" so as not to arouse suspicion. I glanced back as I did. Was it definitely her? I couldn't tell. But she was coming fast. I sped up myself. I checked behind me one more time and then—

SMACK!

At first I thought I'd run into a lamppost. There was a bright red flash and the feeling of my jaw being slammed backward into my skull....

Then I was down, on my back, stunned and not quite

aware of what was happening. I lay there for what felt like several seconds, then managed to roll onto my side....

I tried to focus my eyes, tried to focus my thoughts. At that moment, the bike reached me. It coasted past. It *was* her. It was Reese. She was wearing jeans, sneakers....

But she was not my problem now. Around me stood three men. They were the problem. It was not a lamppost I had run into. It was a human fist.

I got myself up to a sitting position. I massaged my aching jaw with my hand. The men stepped closer. One of them I recognized. It was the old guy from the school bus, the hoarder dude. What the hell was he doing here? We were miles from Topanga.

I struggled to my feet. I leaned against the railing. A seagull squawked. A girl on Rollerblades glided by. The sun had just gone down. It wasn't dark yet, but it was getting there.

"We been lookin' for you," said the older man. The other two were not so old. They were grown men, though. Twenty-five probably. Local guys. Tough-looking, whoever they were.

"Yeah?" I said. "What are you looking for me for?" I was feeling my face. There did not appear to be serious damage. My teeth were all in place, that was the important thing. My nose was bleeding, but it wasn't broken. I didn't think.

"Where's Mugs?" said the old man.

"*Mugs?*" I said, looking at each of them. "How would I know?"

"You were looking for him."

There was no way to deny that. "Someone told me he had puppies," I said, sticking with my original story.

"Puppies?" said the old guy. "What puppies?"

"Some guy told me he was giving away puppies."

"Mugs didn't raise puppies," said one of the younger guys. He glared at me with violence in his eyes. He had a beard and an oily Oakland Raiders cap on his head.

"Who sent you after Mugs?" said the old man.

"Nobody," I said.

They moved closer. The younger guy spoke: "You'd be better off telling us whatever you know. Mugs is gone. And you know where he is."

"I don't," I said, spitting blood. "I swear."

"Then someone you know knows," said the younger guy.

"A guy at the community outreach told me he had puppies. That's it."

"I don't believe you," said the old man.

The younger guy leaped forward and grabbed me. He wrapped one beefy forearm around my neck and then twisted my wrist behind my back. He began pushing it upward.

"You talk or I'm gonna break your arm," he hissed.

The weird thing was, there were people there. People were fishing. People were walking up and down the pier. Like, walking right past us.

The guy kept pushing my arm up my back. He was going to break my arm. Or dislocate my shoulder. Or whatever happens when someone does that.

It hurt. It hurt *a lot.* "Ow! Ow ow ow! Okay! *Okay!*" I gasped.

He let my arm down a few inches and relaxed his grip on my neck. He relaxed in general, which created my one chance for escape.

I stomped my heel down on his toes, as hard as I could. He had light tennis shoes on and I felt a crunch. I might have broken something. He cried out and fell to one side. I tore loose, dashed across the pier, and threw myself over the railing. I cleared it completely and dropped over the other side.

It was a long fall to the water. Fortunately, I'd jumped off that pier before. Diego and I had jumped off it with our surfboards on big surf days when the waves were too intense to paddle out.

This time, though, I hadn't planned my jump, or timed it, or even looked where I was going. I was just falling. I didn't even know if the water was deep enough where I was going to hit.

I landed sideways with a splat. It stung bad. And it really stung when the salt water got into my bloody mouth. By the time I'd found my way back to the surface, I was wide awake with pain and shock and the burn of the salt water.

Above me I could see the three men, staring down at me, talking among themselves, trying to decide what to do. But there was nothing they could do. The ocean current had been strong all week and I was already drifting away from the pier. All I had to do was float and I would be out of reach in a few minutes. Unless they wanted to jump in and try to outswim me. Which they could never do. Like all surfers, I could swim forever.

I drifted north, floating, swimming, staying far out from shore, in case they decided to follow me along the beach. The salt water was buoyant and easy to float in. A hazy crescent moon appeared in the sky above downtown Los Angeles. Two hours later, it was totally dark and I'd drifted halfway to Santa Monica.

When I was sure the beach was deserted, I began to swim for shore. I was careful as I emerged from the surf. I moved slowly, stopping and staying still, to see if anyone might be waiting for me. There didn't seem to be.

I wrung out my wet Vans, which I had jammed into the back of my shorts for swimming purposes. I slipped them on, and made sure I was ready to run, if I needed to. Then I carefully made my way home, using every back alley and secret passageway I knew of.

At Hope's, I crawled over the fence, stripped off my wet clothes, and climbed up my ladder to safety.

Only when I was safe and dry, with the ladder pulled up and my shoulders wrapped in my sleeping bag, did I dare ask myself the questions: *Why had they come all that way to find me? Why did they care so much about Mugs?*

And even more important: *What had happened to Mugs?* I didn't know. That's what scared me the most. I hadn't turned him over to the cops, I'd turned him over to some guy in a track suit.

I felt the murkiness of the situation in my heart.

I didn't like the feeling.

THIRTEEN

I never met the French girls at the Torchlight, but I went there a couple days later, with Diego. It was "'90s Teen Dance Night" and there were a lot of high school kids hanging out. We found our way to the juice bar and got some Cokes. It was a trendy crowd. I could see Goth Reese showing up here, with her lipstick and mascara.

We sat on a bench along the wall and watched people. Diego checked out the "honeys," as he called them. Diego was good with girls. Which made sense—he had four sisters at home and probably a dozen girl cousins. He also had no fear. If he saw a girl he liked, he went right over and started talking. They always seemed to talk right back.

I wasn't so good with that stuff. I mean, I could talk to a girl if she asked me a question, but if I thought she was cute, or thought about her in a romantic way, I'd get too nervous to do anything. The truth was, I hadn't done any of that boy-girl stuff. I'd never been on a date, or even kissed anyone. I'd been too much of a nomad.

Diego saw some of his cousins and went to talk to them. I walked through the crowd by myself. I looked for Reese. When I didn't see her, I went outside and stood on the sidewalk and watched the people walking by. It was a beautiful night, yellow moon in the sky, the smell of ivy and flowers in the air. I looked up and down the street. *Where are you tonight, Reese Abernathy?*

A pair of teenage girls were laughing with two boys at an outside table at the café across the street. I crossed the street to check it out. When I got closer, I got a little jolt of adrenaline. The two guys at the table were the Evil Twins.

I doubted they would remember me from the Nuart, but I changed course anyway, avoiding them and going into the café through a different door. I got a chai latte and sat outside, several tables away.

The amazing thing about the Evil Twins was their faces. They looked *exactly* like what they were: criminals. They had greedy little eyes, pockmarked jaws, devious cheekbones. Even the way they sat, the way they mocked the girls and picked at their fingernails: Their evilness was completely obvious. And yet the girls laughed and giggled and were having a great time. Could they not see the obvious? How could they miss it?

I got a text from Ailis. She asked what I was doing and I texted her I was looking for Reese at "'90s Teen Dance Night."

Come to the Torchlight, I wrote.

A few minutes later, a brand-new white Cadillac Escalade pulled up across the street. The twins abruptly stopped their conversation. Four teenage girls in high heels and extremely tight dresses crawled out. They looked young and dumb and ready to party. They reminded me of Chad Mitchell. Easy money. Which was exactly what the Evil Twins must have been thinking.

"Ladies, it's been real," said the blond twin, standing up.

"Wait," said one of the girls. "Where are you going?"

"It's time to roll," said the dark-haired twin.

"Will you call us?" said a second girl. "Do you want our numbers?"

"We don't do numbers," said the blond twin, walking away.

"But wait!" said the girls.

The dark-haired twin threw his coffee cup casually into the street and followed his partner toward the Torchlight.

The abandoned girls stared after them.

"What's *their* problem?" said the first girl.

"Gawd," said the other. "And we bought them lattes!"

The first girl looked into her bag. "Speaking of which, where's my wallet?" she said.

"Did you leave it inside?"

"I don't know.... It was in here.... I thought it was...."

"Well, look for it."

"I am looking for it!"

I waited until the Evil Twins were inside the Torchlight. Then I crossed the street myself. I reminded myself that they were not my problem. I was here to find Reese Abernathy, not to save dumb girls from obvious criminals.

But inside, I couldn't help but check on their progress. The Cadillac babes had grabbed a large circular booth. They had thrown their purses and coats into a pile in the middle of the round seat. Three of the girls then went to the bar, leaving one girl in the booth with her phone. The twins made their move, approaching her and chatting her up.

Just like the girls at the café, the single girl was charmed and happy to meet two tall and confident guys. She smiled up at them and invited them to join her, which they did. I noticed another phone sitting on the table. *That won't last long*, I thought. But to my surprise, neither twin went for it. Of course not. They didn't want one phone. They wanted all the phones. And all the money. And anything else they could get.

At that moment, Ailis appeared. I grabbed her arm. "See those three girls at the bar?" I said into her ear. "Go tell them they're about to be robbed."

Ailis looked alarmed but did what I asked. I watched her approach the Cadillac babes, who were reapplying their lip gloss and tugging on the bottoms of their stretchy dresses. The girls wouldn't listen to Ailis. They barely acknowledged her. Ailis came back.

"I tried," she said. "They weren't interested."

A moment later, the three girls lurched back to their table on their high heels.

They perked up when they saw the Evil Twins. This was just what they hoped would happen tonight: They would meet some hot guys!

The girls scooted into the circular booth, all of them talking at once. There was a lot of flirting and hair flipping. One of the girls announced to the table: "Some stupid girl just told me I was about to be robbed!"

The whole table laughed. The Evil Twins laughed hardest of all. The blond twin had positioned himself next to the pile of purses. From where I was, I could see his hand gradually move inside one of them while he joked with the girls. A wad of cash came out, which went directly into his pocket.

I turned away. *Better to let nature run its course.* Sometimes it was the only way people learned.

The next day, after some basketball, I swung by the Pizza Slice. Strawberry was there, sitting in the same spot on the curb. She looked dirtier than ever.

"Have you still not taken a shower?" I said to her.

She looked embarrassed and stared at the ground.

"Come on," I said. I lifted her up by the elbow and walked

her down the boardwalk. As we walked, I sniffed the top of Strawberry's head. She stank.

I took her to one of the tourist stalls, where they had cheap towels, cheap beach chairs, cheap everything. I knew the Chinese woman who ran it, Mei Wei. She was no fan of street kids but I'd helped her move some stuff recently, so she owed me.

"My friend here needs a cheap bathing suit," I told Mei. "A bikini."

She found her one. For $6.99.

"And you got any soap?"

Mei could see what I was doing and found an old bar of soap in the back.

I led Strawberry to the back of the shop and handed her the suit. "Change," I said. Mei and I held a big beach towel up in front of her.

Strawberry did it, though she wasn't too happy.

Once she got the bikini on, I handed Strawbs the towel to wrap herself in. She looked miserable with her ratty hair and strange, large eyes. She didn't like being exposed to the open air.

I led her out of the stall and down the boardwalk to the outdoor showers. There, I took off my own shirt, my shoes and socks, and set them aside. Then I got in the shower in my basketball shorts and started lathering up, so Strawberry could see how it was done.

She stood there staring at me. She was shivering. She looked terrified.

I scrubbed my chest, my arms and legs. A surfer was at the other shower, washing off his board and rinsing out his hair. When he left, I pointed for Strawberry to take his place.

"You're up," I said.

She stared at the shower.

"What's the matter?" I asked.

"Is it clean?"

"Of course it's clean. This is California. Everything's clean. Except you."

She stared at the shower.

I went over to her. I gently took the towel away from her. She looked ghostly pale. And she was really dirty. Her feet were black with street grime. Her hair was wild and tangled and so full of grit and dirt I didn't know if we could get it clean.

I led her to the shower and pushed the metal button. When I felt the water was warm, I gradually eased her under it. She gasped when the water hit her. Her eyes opened wide. At that moment, I had the scary thought that Strawberry might be a serious mental case, that she might be too far gone and would live on the street the rest of her life and become a total bag lady. But I didn't let on.

I handed her the soap. She didn't seem to know what to do with it. So I took charge. I held her under the water and lathered her hair up until she looked like a snow lollypop. I scrubbed her skull, digging my fingers in there, using my fingernails. This was pretty brave of me. Who knew what was living in there. It was a miracle she didn't have lice or fleas or worse.

Next were her shoulders and back. Those weren't so bad. Then her arms and hands. Her feet were the worst. They were dirty and cut up, with blisters and broken toenails. I did my best, scrubbing different parts of her feet with a corner of the towel. Then I did her ankles and her calves but stopped at her knees. I didn't want to totally freak her out.

After that, I rinsed her off and got the towel back around her. We sat on a bench, in the sun, and let it bake us dry. Despite her resistance, you could tell she was fascinated by her new state of cleanliness. She kept feeling her hair and looking down at her clean feet. She stared at the back of her hands.

"You need new clothes," I told her.

"I wear children's clothes," she said.

"I believe you," I said, since she was about five feet tall, probably ninety pounds.

Also, I could now see how young she was. She had claimed to be eighteen. But that's what all runaways say, since then you're legal. Now that I could actually see her face and her ears and her shoulders, I knew she was more like fifteen, maybe younger.

"Feels good, being clean?" I said to her.

"Yeah," she said.

"You find yourself a place to live yet?"

"I sleep by the pizza place."

"I know you do," I said, losing my patience again. "That's why you're so dirty!"

She lapsed into silence.

"Strawberry, listen to me. You gotta find a real place. You can't sleep outside. Do you understand that? This isn't some small town. This is Los Angeles, the big city. Bad stuff happens here. It's dangerous."

She said nothing and I realized I was being like an angry parent: ordering her around, making her shower, yelling at her. That was probably the wrong approach.

I walked her back to the Pizza Slice. She got some "clean" clothes out of her backpack, which she kept hidden in an oil drum behind the Dumpster.

I held up the towel again while she changed out of her bathing suit. Then we sat on her curb and ate pizza slices. We barely said a word. I watched the people walking by, keeping an eye out for Reese. Strawberry just sat there.

"Since you sit here all day," I finally said to her, "maybe you could help me out."

I dug three pictures out of my back pocket.

"I've been looking for this girl," I said. "Her name is Reese Abernathy. If you see her on the boardwalk, can you let me know?"

She looked at the pictures a long time. "Who is she?"

"I dunno. Some girl. Ran away from home. Her dad is trying to find her. They asked me to help."

"My parents are trying to find me," said Strawberry.

"I'm sure they are," I said, though it seemed like if Strawberry was this weird, her parents might be even worse. I tried to stay positive. "Even screwed-up parents worry about their kids," I said.

Strawberry seemed to ponder this for a second. But I could never tell what she was thinking, or if she was thinking anything at all.

FOURTEEN

A couple nights later, I was in my treehouse, in my sleeping bag, balancing my laptop on my stomach. I was watching a video about the Civil War. My GED teacher had asked our class about the Civil War, and none of us knew much about it, which freaked her out. So now we were studying that.

I went to the library, and the same guy who always helps me found me a public television series about it. The show used letters and eyewitness accounts, so you could picture what it was really like. The Civil War was a long time ago, before cars or planes or anything really, though they did have cameras. And guns. Which reminded me I still had to figure out where to take a gun-safety class.

"Cali?" called Ailis's voice. It was pretty late, so I was surprised to have company.

I paused the video and pushed my door open. I looked down at her. "Hey," I said.

"Hey," she said back. There was a long silence. "What are you doing?"

"Watching a video about history," I said.

She stood there for a long time. "Can I come up?" she asked.

I wasn't sure that was the best idea. It was hard enough to concentrate on historical stuff without a girl sitting there. "I kinda need to watch this," I said. "It's homework."

She didn't answer. She didn't say anything. She also didn't leave. Something was going on with her.

"All right," I said. "Come up."

She climbed up the ladder and crawled in. She was being weird and quiet.

"What's up?" I said.

"My dad came home," she said.

She had told me about her dad. He was a scary alcoholic. He didn't live with them but he would show up sometimes and it was always bad. First her dad would get drunk and scream at her mom. Then her mom would get drunk and the two of them would scream at Ailis.

I made some space for her on the sleeping pad. She sat there. She couldn't look at me. You could tell from her face she'd been crying.

"Want an orange?" I said, pulling in my bag of oranges.

She shook her head. She wiped her eyes. "What are you watching?" she sniffled.

"A show about the Civil War."

"Is it good?"

"I guess so," I said. "Did you know the South started their own country, and had their own money and their own president?"

"Yes."

"I didn't."

Ailis sat there. She didn't say anything. She looked pretty shaken.

"You okay?" I asked.

"My dad said it was a joke that I go to community college," she said. "He told my mom it's a waste of money and not to pay for me anymore."

"That's not very nice," I said.

She blew her nose. We both sat there in silence.

"Can I watch this with you?" she asked, pointing to my laptop. The screen was paused on an old general with a huge walrus mustache.

"Sure."

"Where do I sit though?"

There wasn't really that much room in the treehouse. The only way for her to watch it was to lie beside me on the sleeping pad.

But we figured it out. The problem was we had to touch a little bit, like, our shoulders, which was no big deal, but it was weird to suddenly be right next to a person and hear them breathing and every time they move you have to move a little too. It reminded me of foster homes, which weren't my fondest memories.

"Is this okay?" she asked, sensing my awkwardness.

"Yeah, sure," I said casually.

I hit play on the video and we both watched. The guy was talking about this one battle where like a thousand soldiers got killed in ten minutes. That was pretty scary. But that was nothing compared to what happened next: Ailis started snoring. Not super loud or anything, but this odd grumbling, rattling sound. She had fallen asleep. Now what was I supposed to do?

So I just lay there, and watched the rest of the episode and then, when it was over, I moved Ailis down a little, and put some of my sleeping bag over her. Then I rolled over so my back was to her so I wouldn't have to listen to her snore.

That was okay. It was warmer with another person there. And she was soft in a way. I mean, it was just my back touching her shoulder, but still, you could feel the girl-ness. You could smell it.

But then, just as I was falling asleep, she woke up suddenly and jerked upright. I'd turned off the light so it was dark and she didn't know where she was. She started to freak out. I reached out to her, to calm her down. But that made it worse. She threw off the sleeping bag and started banging around. She hit her head on the ceiling. She found her way to the door and pushed it open. Without a word, she scrambled down the ladder. I held my laptop open above her so she could see the steps. When she got to the bottom, she ran into Hope's house.

I had no idea where she went. Home maybe. I knew she sometimes slept in her mom's car when her dad was around. So maybe she did that.

The next morning, I went to the basketball courts and shot hoops with Diego. I texted Ailis and asked if she was okay, but she didn't text back. Which was maybe for the best. I didn't know how to help her with her family stuff.

Then Jax showed up. We'd become buddies in GED class and I'd invited him to come play basketball with us. He wasn't very good though. He threw himself around. He had this one move, where he'd cradle the ball in his gut and charge forward, headfirst, which was probably how he got all those scars on his skull. Not from playing basketball, but living his life that way. Headfirst. Crashing forward.

Jax sat down, and Diego and I ended up playing a real game against some guys from El Segundo. It was a good game, an even match. We all played pretty hard. And then something very strange happened.

A girl appeared under the basket.

I didn't notice her at first. The courts are right next to the boardwalk, so random people often stopped to watch us play. But then I drove hard to the hoop and got fouled and I ran right into her. I had to wrap her up, so she wouldn't fall.

And then, with my arms still around her, I looked into her face.

It was Reese Abernathy.

I let her go. I stared at her. She stared at me. And then she smiled.

"C'mon man," yelled the El Segundo guys. "Take the ball out!"

I backed away from her. I went back to the game. I kept playing. And while I did, she stayed right there under the basket, her arms crossed over her chest, watching.

When the game was over, I picked up my T-shirt and wiped the sweat off my face. I approached Reese cautiously.

She put her hand on her hip. She said, "So you're Cali."

"Yeah," I said.

"I heard you're looking for me," she said.

"Uh…" I said. "Yeah. I guess I am." I was not prepared for this. And I was especially not prepared for how beautiful she was. She was gorgeous. Her skin was milky white and her lips were puffy and red and perfectly curved. The pictures had not shown this. And her eyes. They had this glow, this shine to them.

"And what did you want, exactly?" she asked, grinning slightly. She seemed to think this was a boy-girl thing, like maybe I had seen her on the boardwalk and put out the word. She thought I had a crush on her.

"Well, actually..." I said. But I was speechless. I opened my mouth but nothing came out.

Reese and I stepped away from the basketball court. "You want to get a smoothie?" I finally managed to say.

"Okay," she said.

I took her to Seed, the trendy vegan place off Pacific Avenue. It was expensive, but it was known as the "beautiful people" restaurant. Which seemed like the right place to take her.

We went inside. I stared up at the huge chalkboard menu. Reese ordered a wheatgrass juice. I got the Sunrise Surprise.

"How did you find me?" I asked.

"The girl with the pizza sign."

"Oh," I said. "Strawberry."

Reese was looking at the gluten-free biscuits in the display case. "She came right up to me and said you were looking for me. She even knew my name."

"That's pretty good memory, for Strawberry."

"She said you knew things. And I asked her what things, and she said, things about the boardwalk. So then I thought, well, maybe I should meet you."

"I showed her how to take a shower," I said modestly. "So I guess that counts as knowing things."

Reese smiled at that. She seemed to like me. So far.

We took our drinks to a table by the window and sat down. I still couldn't get comfortable with how pretty she was. She looked like a model. Also, I wasn't sure what we were going to talk about. This was a very difficult and unexpected situation.

"So why exactly are you looking for me?" asked Reese, her smile lessening now. She was beginning to sense that something else was going on. I wasn't just some crushed-out boy.

"Well…" I said. What was I supposed to say? Did I have to tell her the truth? It seemed like I did.

"What happened was…" I started. I shifted in my seat. "Well, this guy…he asked me…"

Her expression got sharper, more focused.

"He wanted me to keep an eye out for you," I stammered. "In case you showed up in Venice. He thought you might need help."

The smile vanished off her face. Her eyes narrowed. "What sort of guy?"

"Uh…"

"Like a cop?" she asked.

"No, not a cop…"

As I tried to think of a delicate way to describe Grisham, the memory of his shoulder holster crept into my thoughts.

Reese stared at me with a firm, almost angry expression. I didn't like that. I hated it. I wanted her to be smiling and happy—and *beautiful*—like she had been ten seconds before.

She leaned closer. "*Who* is looking for me?" she said. "Tell me."

"He was a private investigator," I told her.

She stared at me. "Where's your phone?" she said.

I tapped my front pocket, where my phone was.

"Give it to me," she said.

"What?"

"If you want to continue this conversation, let me hold your phone." As she said this, she looked around the restaurant suspiciously. But there were only tourists there: girls in bikini tops, guys in cutoffs.

I reached into my pocket and reluctantly gave her my phone.

She slipped it into her own pocket. She glared at me again. It was chilling, that look. Reese Abernathy, I saw, was a complicated and formidable person. I guess she kind of had to be.

We left the restaurant and walked down Pacific Avenue. "What did he tell you about me?" she said. She was tight-lipped and walking very fast.

"He said you ran away," I answered over the traffic going by. "That you were upset. That you might possibly . . . hurt yourself."

This made her furious. Reese walked even faster, shaking her head as she went. "So they told you about my mother."

I hurried to keep up. "They said your mother committed suicide."

This news seemed to bother her even more.

"Is that not true?" I asked.

"Depends on what your definition of *true* is. But yes,

according to the police, the lawyers, the news media, and my dad's friends, my mother killed herself."

I had no idea how to react to this. What was she suggesting?

We walked for several moments without speaking. "How did you get involved in this?" she asked me.

"In what?"

"In looking for me?"

"I just...I know one of the local cops," I said. "I'm a runaway myself."

"Yeah?" she said. "From where?"

"Omaha, Nebraska."

She turned and studied me, head to foot. "And you came all the way to California? How old were you?"

"Fourteen."

That seemed to impress her. She slowed the pace slightly.

"So you don't have a family?" she asked.

"No."

"How do you live?"

I shrugged. "It's not that hard. It's warm. I got a place to stay. There's food around."

Oddly, she seemed to think about this, as if it could be a possibility for herself.

"But nobody is looking for me," I said. "Not like they're looking for you."

Reese barely seemed to hear this. She seemed to have withdrawn into her own thoughts.

We walked a little longer. Then she stopped and turned

to me. "Listen, Cali, I don't know you. I don't know what your deal is. But I want you to know one thing: My mother *did not* commit suicide."

I nodded.

"My mother…" She paused for a moment, overwhelmed by emotion. "Never mind. It would take too long to explain."

"I have time," I said. "I have all the time in the world."

"The point is, I cannot be found. Or I'll be in danger too. Do you understand? When did you talk to this guy?"

"A couple days ago."

She thought about that. "The truth is," she said, "the people who say they want to help me are exactly the people who are going to hurt me."

"Okay," I said, trying to understand.

She stared down the street and shook her head. "But you don't care about that. You work for them."

"No! But I don't!" I said. "I just started. I'm trying to learn the business. I don't know anything."

She barely heard me when I said this. She was watching the passing cars, waiting for a break in the traffic. Then her eyes locked back onto mine. "I'm gonna ask you, as a personal favor, to give me some time. To give me a head start out of here. To save my own life."

"Of course," I said. "I'll do whatever you want."

"It was nice to meet you, Cali," she said. "You seem like an honorable person. But I'm gonna go now. And I don't want you to follow me."

"I won't," I said. "I swear."

"All right," she said.

I swallowed. At that moment, I knew I would do anything for her. I would help her in any way I could.

Then she turned and ran across Pacific Avenue.

I stayed where I was. Like she told me to.

When she got to the other side, I remembered my phone. "Uh, Reese?" I yelled across the busy street. "What about my phone?"

"You'll get it back!" she shouted.

"How?" I yelled.

But she had turned down a side street. In another moment, she was gone from sight.

FIFTEEN

Strawberry handed me my phone.

"When did Reese give you this?" I asked her. We were standing outside the Pizza Slice.

"Last night," she said.

I tried it. It still worked.

"She's pretty," said Strawberry.

"Yeah, she is," I said.

"Is she rich?"

"Yeah."

Strawberry stared up at me, with her big eyes. "Rich people are dangerous," she said.

"Yeah?" I said.

"When the devil is bored and wants to talk to someone, it's always a rich person he calls. Or someone who wants to be rich."

I glanced down at Strawberry as I put away my phone. "Who told you that?"

"No one."

I was curious to hear more of Strawberry's thoughts, but I had other things to worry about. I was now in a very difficult situation. I was getting paid to find a girl who had just found me. What did I do now? What would a professional private investigator do? I tried to imagine Grisham in this situation. Or Bruce Edwards. They'd probably call whoever hired them and report exactly what happened. And get paid. I was pretty sure of that.

But what about Reese's mother? If she didn't commit suicide, what happened to her? And who caused it to happen? And if Reese herself was in danger, wasn't it my first duty to protect her? No matter what else happened? Wasn't that the whole point?

I called Ailis to see what she thought but she didn't answer. She was probably in class.

In the meantime, I decided to get a haircut. I went to Diego's aunt's hair salon near the marina. I didn't know how such places worked in California. The only barbershop I'd ever been to was in Nebraska, where they played baseball on TV and you read fishing magazines.

This place was all girly and it smelled like nail polish. I went ahead, though. Diego's cousin Maria put me in one of the chairs.

"So you want like, a surfer thing?" she said, since she could see the obvious sun and saltwater damage to my hair.

"I just need it cut," I said. "So it doesn't look so..."

"...like you cut it yourself, with a pocketknife?"

I actually did cut it myself with a pocketknife. "Uh... yeah..." I said.

So then she started combing it. That didn't go well. I felt like Strawberry, having someone try to detangle the rat balls in my hair. I mean, mine weren't as bad as Strawbs's, but I still had some spots that no comb was going to penetrate.

I watched Maria's face in the mirror and suddenly felt embarrassed. Stylish Reese had seen me like this. I must have looked like a wild animal to her.

Maria called her boss over to look at my tangled hair. They both laughed. The boss said: "That's gonna cost extra." But I don't think she meant it.

Finally Maria started cutting. It felt good in a way, the comb moving through my hair, the rhythm of the scissors snipping. It made me feel warm and sleepy, like I was being hypnotized. Maybe it was the feeling of human touch. I didn't get a lot of that. Her hand moving my head forward, pulling it back. The way her soft fingers brushed across my hair, smoothing it, then pulling up a clump to cut it. My eyes started to close. A deep glow began to form in my chest. It was sort of heavenly.

When I was done, Maria turned the chair around so I could look at myself. It looked pretty weird. It looked *girly*, to be honest, all neat and nice and trim. She asked me if I wanted it shorter still, and I said no. It would be hard enough to get used to already. And everyone would make fun of me, of course.

Diego had told me to tip her and I did. But since I didn't know how much, I think I gave her too much. It was worth it though. The whole thing was worth it. I thought I should do this more often. Once a year, at least.

That night I went to GED class. I sat next to Jax, who had a few things to say about my new "college boy" haircut.

"Dude, we're *in* a college," I reminded him, since that's where we were.

That night's class was more discussions about the Civil War. We'd been talking about it all week. The teacher said, "If the South was fighting to preserve their slavery-based economy, what was the North fighting for?"

A couple people tried to answer. Nobody really knew.

I raised my hand. "I watched this video from public TV?" I said. "And according to that, half the soldiers didn't even know what the war was about. It was just a war. So people went. Because a war is like a really intense game of street basketball. It creates an aura that radiates out. And people are attracted to that, especially guys. They don't want to miss out on the action. They want to see it, and be there, and be part of it. They want to get in the game."

Everyone laughed. But I was totally serious. The soldiers

said that exact thing in their letters. None of the politics mattered in the end. It was the thrill of it. The drama. The challenge. There were *people shooting at people*, right down the road. How could you miss that?

"Thank you, Robert," said the teacher. "That's a very mystical way of looking at it."

"Dude, you're *mystical*!" whispered Jax. He gave me a fist bump.

"Anybody else?" said the teacher. "Any other theories other than that wars create auras?"

Everyone laughed at that. But I didn't care. I was right. I totally was.

After class, I met Ailis in the parking lot.

"Do you want to look for Reese?" she said as we got in her car. She was being extra nice now, to make up for her freak-out in the treehouse.

"Actually..." I said, putting my seat belt on. "I found her."

"You found her?" gasped Ailis. "When?"

"Yesterday."

"Where was she?"

"She came to the basketball courts."

"She came *to you*?"

"I know," I said. "It was very strange."

Ailis stared at me with wonder.

"She told me her side of the story," I continued. "It turned out to be more complicated than I thought."

"Like how?"

I took a long breath. "She said her mom didn't commit suicide."

"But she did!" said Ailis. "I looked it up myself. There were articles about it online."

"She seems to think something else happened," I said.

"Something else? Like what?"

"She didn't say. It sounded like her dad might be involved."

"She thinks her *dad* killed her mom?" said Ailis in disbelief.

"Maybe so," I said. "I know. It sounds crazy."

"That's impossible!" said Ailis. "That's like something in a movie!"

I looked out my window. "I know."

Ailis thought about this. We both thought about it.

"Do you believe her?" said Ailis.

"I don't know what to believe," I said. "It does sound crazy. But when she told me...I believed her. She has this way about her. She's very open. And honest. And kinda vulnerable in a way. You want to help her."

Ailis frowned slightly when I said that.

I began tapping the door lightly with my knuckle. "The thing is, what do I do about Grisham? I can't take his money if I'm not going to help him."

"You want to take yourself off the case?" asked Ailis.

"What else can I do?"

"Find out the truth!"

"And how am I gonna do that?"

Ailis didn't know. I didn't know.

"I'll call him tomorrow," I said.

"What are you gonna say?"

"I'm gonna quit. I can do that. It's just a job."

"Are you sure?" asked Ailis.

I nodded. But the truth was, I had no idea.

I could barely sleep that night. Would I be breaking some private-investigator code by quitting the Reese case? Would I ever get hired again? This was my dream job. This was the only thing I wanted to do.

Early the next morning, I skateboarded to the beach. A nice swell from the southwest had come up and the early-morning surfers were hurrying toward the beach. I wished I was going surfing. That seemed so easy, so uncomplicated.

I cruised the boardwalk. The stalls were just opening up—the cheap sunglasses places, the surfboard rental. I wondered where Reese was at that moment. But I was glad I didn't know. I didn't want to know.

And then in the midst of my worries, I had a different thought: Where was Mugs?

I hated how that felt so unresolved. It occurred to me that this was the reality of being a private investigator. You might never know what the exact story was, or who was telling the truth, or what actually happened to the people you found or worked for.

That led to another thought: What if I didn't have the stomach for the private-investigator business? What if I was like one of those Civil War soldiers, attracted to the aura of war? It sounded so fun and exciting when you're sitting at home. But now I was here, in the thick of it, experiencing the reality. And it wasn't fun at all.

I played hoops with Jojo and some other people that afternoon. Jojo was just shooting. No driving. No dunks. Just midrange jump shots. He made every single shot he took. It was a nice workout, a quiet game. Jojo could have that effect on you. Playing ball with him, just being in his presence, it calmed your mind. It reminded you that everything was basically okay.

As I sat on the bleachers, waiting for the next game, my phone rang. It was an LA number I didn't recognize. I took the call. "Hello?"

"Hey, it's me," said Reese.

"*Reese?*" I said. I turned away from the basketball court.

"I was wondering if you'd told my father's henchman where I was."

"No," I said. "I haven't said anything. I was about to call the guy who hired me."

"And do what?"

"Quit."

"Really?" she said.

"Well yeah, what else can I do?"

"You could take their money and turn me in."

"I would never do that."

"Well, thank you," she said, a new warmth in her voice. "That says a lot about you as a person."

"I think in the future," I said, "I'm only gonna take jobs where I know what is actually happening, who's the good guy, who's the bad guy."

"Are there many cases like that?"

"I don't know," I said. "But those are the ones I want. I don't like it when things get complicated."

"But isn't everything pretty complicated when you get right down to it?"

"I don't know," I said.

"I think it is."

"Well, you would know, I guess."

"What does that mean?"

"Just..." I said. "You seem pretty smart about stuff."

"Me?" She laughed. "You're the one who's smart about stuff. Talk about street smarts. You get people to pay you to hang around and shoot baskets!"

I hadn't thought of it that way, but she was right.

"You want to hang out later?" she said. "I owe you a smoothie."

This completely threw me. I had assumed she was three states away and moving fast. "Like where? In Venice?"

"Of course in Venice. Where did you think I was?"

"I assumed you were...gone."

"I'll meet you at six. But it's gotta be someplace out of the way."

I told her to meet me at the Milk Bar Cafe, on Washington.

She was late. I guess that made sense. I got a latte and sat at an outside table. I waited. And waited.

She finally appeared, walking fast down the sidewalk. She was wearing a yellow summer dress and lipstick. She saw me and nodded from behind her big sunglasses. "Let's walk," she said.

I jumped out of my seat and followed her down the sidewalk.

We moved along through the crowd. "Can I have a sip of your coffee?" she asked me.

I handed her my paper cup. She drank some and handed it back. I noticed the lipstick marks on the lid. They were the exact color of blood.

We walked toward the pier and ended up on the beach, walking along the water. Naturally, I wanted to hear more about her family situation. What really happened to her mother? And if someone else was involved, who was it? But she didn't want to talk about that. Instead, she wanted to hear about Nebraska and how I got from there to California at fourteen. I was like, why would you want to hear about that? But she insisted. And who could deny Reese Abernathy anything? Not me.

So I did my best, telling about my birth family: my father

who disappeared and my mother, a nurse, who was killed on an icy road trying to help at the scene of a car accident. Then my years in social services, my weird foster families, my horrible first year of high school, and the moment I realized I had to get out of Nebraska. And so began the planning, the scheming, and eventually my escape...

After my story, Reese told about her life. Growing up back east. The move to California. How her supposedly "upstanding" father was unpredictable and ruthless and sometimes violent at home. He once pushed her mother off a chairlift in Colorado, and then claimed it was an accident. They moved around. Reese was always changing schools. Nothing stayed the same. They'd give her a horse, they'd take it away. They'd start her with dance lessons then stop. The happy life she imagined for herself, which seemed so easily within her reach, never materialized.

"So what are you gonna do?" I finally asked. We had stopped at the water's edge to watch the pelicans skim across the surface.

"I don't know. What do you think I should do?"

"Can you prove anything about your mom?" I asked.

"Not really."

"You've got no proof at all? Nothing you could show the police?"

"The police do whatever my father tells them to do."

I nodded with sympathy. "So you're stuck."

"I'm worse than stuck," she said. "I'm one girl against a

small army of very well-paid detectives. They're gonna follow me forever."

I stood, pondering this.

"Thank god I found you," she said, her voice softening.

"What can I do, though?"

"You can keep me sane."

"How am I going to do that?"

She looked at me funny then. She said, "By *this*. By talking. By hearing about your life."

"Does that really help?"

"Yes, Cali, that really helps. Why do you think there's therapists?" She looked at me closer then, like she couldn't believe how clueless I was.

Then she got this really practical look on her face. She pulled her hair back and knotted it behind her head. "Come here," she said, stepping forward in the sand.

"What?" I said.

She grabbed my elbows and pulled me toward her. "This is called a *hug*," she said. She put her arms around me and pulled me close. It was very innocent. It was like the hugs you get in foster care when your fake parents tell you to hug your fake brothers and sisters.

"How does that feel?" she said.

"Okay."

"Just okay?"

"I've hugged people before," I said. "I'm not a space alien."

But inside, I was freaking out. It wasn't that Reese wasn't

a girl any guy would dream of hugging. It was just so sudden. And so confusing. I was still supposedly looking for her. And being paid to do it.

She settled into the hug a little more. She gripped me more tightly. It did feel pretty amazing.

"Cali?" she whispered into the side of my neck.

"Yeah?" I said.

"You're supposed to hug me back."

"Oh," I said, quickly putting my arms around her. "Sorry."

SIXTEEN

The next day, I called Grisham. And I lied. I was not the best liar it turned out.

"What ya got for me?" he said.

"Nothing," I said, my voice tightening. "I've been everywhere. If she was here, she's gone."

"Well, keep at it. I'll switch you over to my assistant, she'll reimburse you for expenses."

"Uh, actually," I said, "I wanted to talk to you about that."

"Sorry kid, we can't give you any more money."

"It's not that. It's that I'm...I'm going away for a while. I think you should get someone else."

"What?"

"I'm leaving town. So I can't work for you anymore."

"You're barely working for me now, son. And I'm paying you good money."

"Right, I know. But I kinda want to chill out for now...."

"You want to *chill out*?"

"Right, like, I'm taking classes and stuff. I don't feel like—"

"I thought you were going out of town?"

"No, I am, I just..."

"And now you don't *feel like working on this anymore*? Kid, let me explain something to you. You don't just come and go on these jobs. You don't just do it when you feel like it. You're part of this. This isn't a *game*."

I firmed myself up. "Listen, Mr. Grisham. I'm quitting. I'm off the case. If you want your money back, I'll give it back."

There was a long, ominous pause. "No," he said. His voice had a slippery, devious tone to it now. "That won't be necessary. I'm just curious though. What happened that made you change your mind?"

"I don't like this sort of thing."

"What sort of thing is that?"

"Situations that I don't completely understand."

There was another long, dangerous silence. "All right," came his voice again. "Consider yourself relieved of duty. Where do I send the last check?"

"I don't want any more money," I said.

"Kid, I have to send it to you. It's on the books....Let's

see here...." There was a pause. "You want it care of Hope Stillwell? 137 Garland Street? Venice, California? Is that right?"

"Yeah," I said.

"And you still live in the treehouse in the back?"

"Yeah," I said.

"All right then, the check is in the mail."

I hung up. Then I stopped for a second.

How did he know about the treehouse?

That night, I had a vivid dream. I was in a police station and Mugs was there, being questioned about a crime he swore he didn't commit. Everyone knew he was lying and it was announced he would get the death penalty. He cried and begged to the police but they took him to the execution room anyway. I watched them drag him down the hallway. They were going to chop off his hands for some reason. And then electrocute him. Just when they closed the door, I heard him yell my name. "Cali!" he cried. "Tell them the truth! Tell them the truth!"

I jerked awake, my face cold and damp. I sat up and turned on my light. It took several minutes to calm myself down.

I texted Ailis, even though it was three in the morning. She didn't answer. I stared at the plywood walls of my treehouse. They reminded me of the insides of a coffin. I texted Reese. I didn't want to tell her about my creepy dream so I wrote:

*I'm officially off your case. Let me know if I can help in
any way.*

She wrote back immediately, even though it was so late:

Thank you. Where are you?

I wrote back:

In my treehouse.

She wrote:

You have a treehouse? Are you serious? Can I come see it?

I wrote back:

*Your dad's people know where I live. They might be
watching it.*

She wrote:

*You're smart. It's a good thing someone is. Some other
time then.*

On Tuesday, I went to GED class. Afterward, Jax and I
hung out at his place. He lived in his uncle's garage. It was a

nice setup, lots more room than I had, with space heaters and a TV and a couch to sleep on. The only problem was the uncle, who was an ex-military guy. He had all this Navy Seals crap. He'd have a couple beers and out would come the combat knives and the surveillance gear and the night vision goggles.

I went home after that. It was always weird to go from "Here's how you stab a guy in the neck" at Jax's house to "Here's how you cleanse your chakras" at Hope's.

I let myself in. Hope and everyone were asleep, and I crept through to my treehouse. I lay down for a few minutes, but as soon as the silence settled in around me, I knew sleep would be impossible. It was Mugs. I was going to dream about him again.

So I got up and climbed back down my ladder and hit the boardwalk with my skateboard. It was after midnight now. The shops were locked up tight. Most of the street people were asleep. I pushed up to a decent speed and coasted along. I was riding a new longboard I'd just bought. It rolled like a Cadillac, smooth, silent, effortless. I'd bought some new clothes, too, and new shoes, which I was wearing. All of this so I could go into nicer places like the youth hostel, or the Nike store, without drawing attention to myself. So I could pursue my investigations. So I could be, in a way, invisible.

That was *if* I still had a chance to be a private investigator. The Mugs thing was weighing on my mind. And the situation with Reese hadn't turned out so great either. If I kept quitting in the middle of jobs, I wouldn't last very long in the business.

❂   ❂   ❂

I passed the homeless people camped out on the boardwalk, most of them zipped up in their sleeping bags, a few still awake, their heads propped up, reading old paperbacks in the dark, or just lying there, alone in the world, staring into the night sky, the sounds of surf in the distance.

I cruised to the north end of the boardwalk and then decided to continue up to Santa Monica. That required traveling another two miles on the deserted bike path. I sped up, rolling easy on my brand-new polyurethane wheels, feeling the comfort of my ninety-dollar skate shoes.

I'd gone about a half mile or so when I sensed something behind me. I looked back. I didn't see anything. I kept going, pushing a little harder, cruising alongside an empty beach parking lot.

A moment later, I sensed something again...movement...was someone behind me...?

I looked back. Nothing.

I kept going, but I kept my speed up with steady pushes. I remembered this guy once telling me that in terms of street survival, *speed* is always the best weapon. Better than a gun, a knife, martial arts, whatever. The guy who can't be caught is the safest.

I looked back. This time I did see something. Two people far behind me. Skaters. They were cruising too. They did not appear to be hurrying. Or following me. They were just there. They would push a bit, coast a bit. They were lanky guys and pretty fast. They were keeping up with me, more or less.

I pushed hard and coasted too, letting my clean new wheels do the work. I watched my shadow stretch out ahead of me, and then back, as I passed beneath the parking lot lights. I stood sideways and made myself thin, to decrease wind resistance. I glanced back behind me. They were still there. They were staying with me. And since I was moving at top speed, I knew their presence was not as innocent as it seemed.

I started looking around for places to bail, places to get off the bike path and make a run for it, toward civilization. But I was now in the no-man's-land between Venice and Santa Monica. On my right were large empty parking lots and the steep dirt hill that led up to Main Street. On my left was a hundred yards of sand and then the ocean. If I ditched the bike path and tried to run for it, they'd see me. And if they could skate this fast, they could probably run pretty fast too.

I glanced back again. This time the light was better. I couldn't see their faces, but something about the motion of their bodies, of their silhouettes...and then I knew...and a chill went through my body....

The Evil Twins.

They were now just thirty yards behind me, and gaining a little with every push.

SEVENTEEN

They wouldn't kill me. They'd just knock me around a little. The Chad Mitchell treatment. It was the board they'd want, and my shoes, and the hundred bucks in cash I unfortunately had in my wallet.

I kept pushing. I could see the lights of the Santa Monica Pier up ahead of me. But I'd never make it that far. Another big parking lot came up on my right. I felt something then, an instinctual urge to make my move now.

I turned sharply to my right and took off, pushing frantically across the uneven parking lot asphalt. The twins were caught off guard, for a moment. But they both made the turn and in a few seconds they were right behind me again. They'd actually gained on me.

So much for my instincts.

I pushed hard and kept my speed up. My wheels were hitting bits of sand, little rocks, stuff my big expensive wheels worked well on. They were on shorter boards, had smaller wheels, and yet I couldn't seem to gain any ground.

Then a lucky break: One of them hit something. He fell off his board and then had to run back to retrieve it. That gave me a little breathing room.

I developed a strategy now. I would ditch my board at the edge of the parking lot and try to outclimb them up the dirt cliff to Main Street. They'd get my board but I wouldn't take a beating and I'd still have my cash and my shoes and my wallet.

I pushed with everything I had to get across that parking lot. When I reached the far side, I crouched down, bent my knees, and let my board hit the concrete curb at full speed. I flew off it, breaking into a full sprint. I hit the dirt cliff and scrambled upward. This all worked pretty well, and yet, halfway up, the two of them were still right at my heels. The closest one, the blond twin, was hardly ten feet behind me. They were good climbers, it turned out. They were apparently good at everything.

I tried evasive climbing. I zigzagged up the cliff. I was taking crazy risks, clawing my way up the steepest parts. But I couldn't lose them. Just twenty feet from the top, the blond twin lunged upward and caught my foot. It was like an iron shackle had been locked onto me. I kicked at him, twisted, spun to get away. His grip was unbreakable.

I started to slip and I grabbed for a bush. The dark-haired twin came up beside me. He grabbed the back of my pants. I struggled to hold on but they had me now. Far below, I could see the black asphalt of the parking lot.

"Okay!" I barked, clinging to the bush. "You got me! I give up!"

I looked into the face of the dark-haired twin beside me. He smiled in his creepy way.

"I'll give you whatever," I said, breathing hard from the climb. "Just don't throw me down."

"Dude," he said, smiling. "You made us climb all the way up here. We have to throw you down."

It wasn't actually a cliff. It was more like a very steep hill.

They threw me down it.

I rolled and tumbled and landed on the hard parking lot surface. They were on me instantly. They were total pros, a few kicks, a couple punches, and then they cleaned me out. My wallet. My phone. My loose change. My belt. My new shoes. My board. Even my hoodie, which, thanks to my fall, had a big rip in the elbow.

When it was over, they got back on their boards and skated leisurely away, across the parking lot, carrying my stuff. I stayed where I was, rolled up on my side. When I was sure they were gone, I slowly turned over and sat up. I spat blood onto the gravel. I felt my mouth and my jaw. My teeth were okay, thank god. I checked the rest of my face, my hands, my fingers. Everything hurt, but nothing was broken.

I struggled to my feet and took a deep painful breath. Then I rolled off my socks, stuck them in my pockets, and started the long walk home, barefoot.

EIGHTEEN

The next morning, I had a huge black eye when I showed up at the basketball courts. Naturally, Jax and Diego wanted to hear what happened. So I told the story.

Some of the older guys started nodding immediately. They knew about the Evil Twins. One dude said they were from Long Beach and they rotated around to different beach areas to steal stuff and mug people. Another guy thought they were brothers. Another person said they used to steal cars for a guy, who sent them on container ships to the Philippines. Whoever they were, the twins were notorious. "If you ever encounter them..." one latecomer warned us.

"Oh, I've encountered them," I said, pointing at my swollen face.

So then everyone got pissed off that they'd mugged me.

People said we should hunt them down and show them who controlled Venice Beach. Everyone except Jojo, who interrupted the macho talk and said we needed to forgive. "Always forgive," he told me, gripping my forearm. "Always forgive."

After that we got back to basketball and everyone forgot about the Evil Twins. I had Jojo on my team for several games and we smoked everyone, which made me feel better.

That afternoon, Jax, Diego, and I went to get pizza. Strawberry was there, sitting on the curb with her PIZZA SLICE $1.99 sign, staring into space.

We got some slices and went to the chess tables. Strawberry and Jax had never met and they stared at each other a lot, neither of them being good talkers. Strawberry noticed Jax's numerous head scars and moved closer to look. She would touch one, and Jax would explain how he got it. "A guy hit me with a hammer," he would say. Or "I fell off a train in New Mexico." Or "I got in a fight with a rack of Hostess Cupcakes." It was pretty funny. Both Strawberry and Jax had head issues, it turned out. Strawberry said she picked at her scalp when she got nervous. She showed us the numerous scabs and scars on her own head. So then Jax saw a dog tied up with one of those plastic cones around his head, and he snuck over and took the cone off, and tried to put it on Strawberry. Everyone thought this was hilarious except the guy who owned the dog.

Later, sitting around in the grass, Strawberry started

hitting Jax. Not hard, just every few minutes, she would reach over and punch him in the gut, or in the shoulder. Could Strawberry like Jax? She sure liked punching him. And Jax didn't mind. Sometimes he'd catch her arm and do a slow-motion karate move on her, narrating in a movie voice: "The feeble blow is neutralized and countered with a lethal face smash...."

The two of them had a lot of fun together. Diego and I both said how it was the first time we ever saw Strawberry laugh.

Ailis and I went to another alien-invasion movie a couple nights later. *Underground Attack Force*, it was called. The basic story was that aliens embedded special pods in our planet ten thousand years ago. Now, after lying dormant all that time, the earth had reached a certain temperature and the aliens were waking up. Naturally, they started blasting the crap out of everything. There was some good urban destruction, including downtown Los Angeles getting melted into a concrete soup by a radium particle beam. I hardly ever went to downtown LA. But I saw it get destroyed a lot in movies.

Afterward, Ailis and I drove around. We talked about the Reese case. Had I done the right thing, by quitting? We talked about other issues of the private-investigator business. Like which cases you should take and which cases you should avoid. And how much you need to know before you took a job. And what sort of agreement you needed to have with the people you worked for.

Ailis was a good person to have this conversation with. She had a logical mind. And a good business sense. She helped me see things in a clearer way.

"You should be my partner," I said at one point, sort of joking, but sort of not.

Ailis looked over at me. "Would you want me to?"

She was serious.

"I don't know," I said, shrugging. "Would you want to be?"

We both kind of hesitated. The idea of us being *together* in any way was very difficult. For both of us.

"I've thought about it," she said finally. "It seems like you would need another person."

It was weird because one part of me was like, *No way do you want Ailis in your business*. But another part of me saw the advantages. She was smart. She was good on computers. She had a car. Plus, I could talk to her about things. That was the best part. Someone to bounce ideas off. Or just to have ideas in the first place.

"Do you think we could work together?" she said.

"We've done okay so far," I answered.

"I have to admit," she said, staring at the steering wheel, "since you told me about Reese, that's all I think about."

"I know. Me too."

"I like having a problem to solve," she said. "Something to think about. Something that actually matters."

"Yeah," I said. "I know what you mean. I hate that I don't have a new person to look for. I'm so bored right now."

Ailis and I both fell silent.

"We could try it," I said.

"Yeah, we could see how it goes," she said.

We both sat there for a moment, unsure of what to say or do next.

The following morning, I was heading to the Venice library to study for my first GED exam. I'd never really studied for anything before and I told Hope about my class during breakfast. She gave me some pointers.

When I finally left, I hopped on my old crappy skateboard and cruised toward the library. That's when I saw the white Mercedes parked at the end of our street. The driver's-side door opened as I got closer. An older man got out. He was wearing a light gray suit, with a white handkerchief in the pocket. He stepped into the street in front of me and held up his hand for me to stop.

I did, but I kept back. There was something about the guy. For one thing, he was too well dressed for this neighborhood.

"You're Robert," he said to me, noticing that I was keeping my distance.

"People call me Cali," I said, checking the Mercedes to see if he was alone. He appeared to be.

"Okay, Cali," he said. "I didn't mean to alarm you. I was wondering if we could talk."

"And who are you?" I said, doing a quick scan of the rest of the street, and behind me.

He smiled pleasantly. "My name is Richard. Richard Abernathy. I'm Reese's father."

NINETEEN

I didn't answer right away. It took me a second to process what he'd said.

Mr. Abernathy seemed to understand this and stood patiently beside his car. It was very shiny. It was brand-new.

"Have you found Reese yet?" I asked, still not moving.

"No. We haven't. That's what I wanted to talk to you about. Can we go somewhere?"

We went to Seed, the same place I took Reese. We both ordered iced teas and sat at one of the tables by the window. I kept my mouth shut and waited for him to do the talking.

"I wanted you to know," he told me, stirring his tea, "I spoke with Reese last night. She called. I was so relieved to hear her voice...."

I sat. I waited.

"She told me where she was. Not the exact location. But she said she was here in Los Angeles, and that she had met one of my people, a young person, who I assume is you, since you recently quit the search."

I started to offer an excuse but he stopped me.

"No, no, I understand," he said. "Grisham told me. That is entirely in your rights. And I'm sure when you met Reese, she persuaded you that she was not a common runaway, that she was in danger or was the victim of some conspiracy, or some such thing. I'm sure it was thoroughly convincing. I don't blame you in the least."

I watched him closely.

"You see, the thing about Reese is"—he paused, looking pained—"she has a condition. Different doctors call it different things. But the basic idea is: She lives in a kind of fantasy world. She does not completely connect with reality at times. And she is, unfortunately, going through one of those times right now."

Richard Abernathy sighed and took a drink of his iced tea. He was balding on the top of his head. But on the sides, his hair was thick and speckled gray. He had solid features and appeared deeply confident in himself, though at the moment he was obviously in distress over the loss of his daughter. He spoke carefully about her, as if it was crucially important that he keep the facts straight in his own mind.

"It appears her latest idea is that I am somehow responsible for her mother's death. And maybe I am, in some way," he said, looking into his tea. "But her version of it. Or her *versions*, I should say. Whatever she told you. That is not the reality of the situation...."

"You're saying she's a liar?"

He shook his head sadly. "Not a liar. God no. It's just that...like for instance, one Christmas, when she was six years old...somehow she decided she had a brother, and that he had died in a fire. All Christmas she talked about it. She would tell our dinner guests, she told her teachers, she told a policeman at the mall. She had a brother, who had died in a fire, under mysterious circumstances. But in fact, she had no brother. She never had a brother. We told her that. We told her over and over."

I maintained my silence.

"As for my wife," he continued, "she was a lot like Reese in that way. That's why I fell in love with her. She was a dreamer. A visionary. Incredibly creative and talented. She had a similar way of reinventing the world, making it more the way she thought it should be, as opposed to the way it actually was. This can be a great quality in a partner. It gives you the feeling that anything is possible. Of course, the doctors have their own terminology for these things: delusion syndrome...personality disorder...disassociation...I don't like to think in those terms. To me it's the price you pay for an extraordinary mind. The point is, Reese is not well. She needs to be under the care of her doctors. I consider her to be in great danger right now."

I watched Mr. Abernathy closely as he spoke. I watched his face. I watched his eyes. How did you know if someone was lying? I didn't know. How did you know if someone was telling the truth? I didn't know that, either.

"What do you want from me?" I asked.

"She trusts you," he said. "I could hear it in her voice. I think she'll contact you again. Or maybe you can contact her. In either case, I beg of you, call me. Help me find her. I'll pay you twice what you were getting before. I'll give you a bonus. Whatever you want, it's yours. And I won't say anything to Grisham. He will continue his search as well, but you can report directly to me." He slid a business card across the table toward me.

I took the card. I held it in my hands. I considered my situation.

Then I cleared my throat. "Here's what I'm going to do," I told him. "If I can help her, I will. But I'm not working for you and I'm not taking any money."

Abernathy looked confused. "But why not?"

"Because I don't know who's telling the truth."

"What do you mean? *I'm* telling the truth. Reese is a sick girl. She needs help!"

He dug into his inside coat pocket and pulled out some papers. "These are doctor's evaluations. The best doctors in San Francisco!"

I took the papers but I didn't look at them.

"She trusts you," said Abernathy, pleading. "She told me

that. You could potentially save her. She's a beautiful, talented young woman. And with the right treatment, she could live a normal life. She could be a person like you, someone who overcomes their circumstances and makes something of themselves...."

I was surprised by this personal flattery. Richard Abernathy had done his homework.

"If I don't find her," he continued, "who knows what will happen to her. Down here? In this world? Among these people...?" he gestured out the window at the Venice locals, his whole body cringing with disgust.

We both sat in silence for several moments. Mr. Abernathy became lost in thought. It was like he'd forgotten I was there. What if he was the one who was disconnected from reality?

I stood up. He started to stand too, but I motioned for him to stay where he was.

"So you'll call me, if you see her again?" he asked.

"I told you. I'll help if I can. But what form that will take, I'm gonna make my own call."

"But I'm her father! She's a child! She has serious mental health issues!"

"Lots of people have issues," I said. "That doesn't mean they aren't telling the truth."

Out of the restaurant, I headed for the boardwalk. My heart was pounding in my chest. *Now what the hell was I sup-*

posed to do? I reached for my phone—my new replacement phone—but I hadn't put Ailis's number in it yet.

I went to the Pizza Slice, where Strawberry was standing in the middle of the boardwalk, holding up her PIZZA SLICE $1.99 sign. Jax sat on the curb a few feet away.

I sat down beside Jax. Then I collapsed, lying back on the dirty concrete and putting my forearms over my eyes.

"What's your problem?" Jax asked me.

"I'm having a professional crisis," I said.

"Dude, you have a profession? Besides sucking at basketball?"

"Cali finds people," said Strawberry.

"What?" Jax said. "Who does he find?"

"Runaways," said Strawberry.

Jax turned to me. "No way."

"I helped him," said Strawberry. "I found Reese Abernathy."

Jax looked at both of us. "Who's Reese Abernathy?"

"She's rich," said Strawberry. "And she's beautiful."

"She is?" asked Jax. "Well, where the hell is she?" He kicked my foot.

I sat up and sighed. "I don't know, and I don't care," I said. "I'm off the case. I'm done with these rich and powerful types. You can never tell who's lying and who's telling the truth."

"I told you," said Strawberry.

I shook my head. But I smiled too. Because Strawbs was right. She did tell me.

TWENTY

Then one day Jax showed up at the basketball courts carrying an unusually large pillow, still in the packaging. We stopped playing and watched Jax lay it down carefully on the bleachers. "Birthday present," he said, before we asked.

"For who?" I said.

"Strawbs."

The rest of us had not known it was her birthday. But Jax knew. He really liked Strawberry, it seemed. He was always hanging around the Pizza Slice, showing up with little presents, like miniature colored marshmallows, which he stole from the Beach Mart and which were Strawberry's favorite food. He would do anything to make her laugh. Like walk around with a melting ice-cream cone stuck upside down on his head. Or demonstrating how to catch seagulls with your bare hands—he actually caught one and almost got his face pecked off.

What Strawbs thought of Jax was more of a mystery. You could put in a lot of Strawberry time and never really know what went on in her head. "She's the strangest girl I ever met," said Diego. For me the question was: Where did she go when she spaced out? Like you'd see her sometimes, and she'd be staring into space like she does, completely oblivious to her surroundings, and you'd be like: Where is she right now? What's it like there?

We continued our basketball game. We let Jax play, which was not the greatest idea since he can barely dribble and mostly crashes into people. But we got through it without anyone getting hurt.

Afterward, Jax rinsed his stubble head in the drinking fountain. Then he picked up his enormous pillow. "Let's go find Strawberry!" he said.

Diego and I went with him. She was sitting on the curb, in her usual spot.

"Hey, Straw-girl. I got you something," said Jax, very pleased with himself.

He handed her the pillow, which was almost as big as she was.

"Oh," she said, gripping it in her small arms. "What is it?"

"It's a pillow!" he said.

She looked more closely and then saw the little sticker on the wrapping that said: PILLOW.

"Oh," she said.

"That's just part of the present," said Jax. "There's another part. But it's on Sixth Street."

So Jax led the group of us on a walk to Sixth Street. We arrived at a house there that I'd never seen before. Nobody seemed to be home. We walked around to the side, and Jax reached over the fence and opened the gate.

This made me nervous. Letting yourself into random backyards was a good way to get shot on Sixth Street.

"And this," said Jax, playing the tour guide, "is my uncle's girlfriend's house." He led us into the small yard. One of those portable toolsheds stood near the back of it, next to a swing set. The shed had been fixed up to look like a large dollhouse. Someone had painted shutters by the windows and flowers along the base of it.

Jax went to it and opened the door and motioned for us to look inside. We did. There was a good-sized room in there. It was clean and swept. Along one wall was a cot. And on the cot there were some blankets folded up.

Jax took the pillow from Strawberry and ducked inside. He laid the pillow at the end of the cot. "And that...goes there!" he said with a flourish.

None of us understood. Strawberry least of all.

"This is yours," Jax told Strawberry. "You can stay here."

"I can?" said Strawberry.

"My uncle's girlfriend lives in the house. She says you can use the shed whenever you want. You can live here."

I got it then. Strawberry had found her treehouse.

"And there's a little shower thing on the side of the house," said Jax. "You can take showers."

"And you can stash your clothes," I said.

"You can *wash* your clothes," added Diego.

"I would live here?" said Strawberry. "In this?"

"Yes," said Jax. "Right here. And my uncle's house is one block down. That's where I live. You can come over whenever you want. You can watch TV."

Strawberry stood there, speechless.

"Try out your pillow," said Diego.

"Yeah," said Jax. "Lie down."

Strawberry touched the cot. It was one of those Army Navy ones, pretty big, pretty comfortable. She turned and lowered her tiny butt onto it.

Jax was beaming. He was so happy. Jojo was always telling us that you had to give of yourself. That was the only true happiness, doing something for another person. Jax was experiencing that right now. He was so happy he could barely stand it.

Strawberry slowly put her full weight on the cot, then turned and lay down on it. Her eyes were wide open, but she rested her head against the pillow and let her head sink into it.

"Look at that," said Diego. "You're a doll in a dollhouse!"

Everyone smiled at that. Even Strawberry. But then her big eyes got soft and wet and we all realized she was overwhelmed and confused and she didn't know how to respond to this.

"C'mon," said Jax, suddenly embarrassed himself. "Let's go look at the shower."

He and Diego went out. Strawberry sat up.

"I never know how to act when people do things for me," she said to me quietly.

"Just go along with it," I said. "Do it for them. Let them feel good."

That night, I had another dream about Mugs. In this one, I was walking along the boardwalk and I heard someone call my name. I looked down, and at my feet there was a grate over a deep storm drain. That's where the voice was coming from.

I got down on my knees and looked through the grate. Ten feet below me, there was another grate. Mugs was trapped beneath it. I could see his hands gripping the bars as he told me, in a strangely calm voice, that water was coming up beneath him.

"I need your help with this, Cali," he said. "This is not something I can deal with right now."

I could see the water all around him. It was rising fast. It reached his chest, his shoulders, his neck....

"I know we've had disagreements in the past," he said, his face now pressed against the bars, "which I am willing to discuss. But right now, what I need from you is a commitment—"

The water rose over his face and covered him completely. And yet his mouth continued to move, bubbles now coming out instead of words.

"Don't worry," said a stranger behind me, who had stopped to watch. "Nothing he says after he's dead can be used in a court of law."

I jerked awake, terrified. I threw off my covers. I tumbled out of the treehouse, sliding down the ladder half dressed. When I landed in the grass my whole body was shaking. I climbed over Hope's fence and ran into the street. I didn't know what I was doing or where I was going. I didn't even have my shoes on.

I found myself walking toward the beach. It was very late, 4 AM probably. Venice was dead quiet and you could hear the soft rush of waves in the distance.

I walked along the boardwalk, beside the long lines of sleeping bags and hobos and dogs and tents. All those people without a home, but at least they could sleep at night.

I came to the tattoo parlor that Jojo lived behind, and I suddenly realized why I had come out here. I walked around to Jojo's little cardboard shack. It was very small. You could see his bare feet sticking out one end of it.

I bent down. "*Jojo*," I whispered.

He grumbled and shifted.

"*Jojo!*" I whispered again.

He lifted his head and looked out at me.

"Who is that?" he asked sleepily.

"It's me, Cali," I whispered. "I gotta talk to you."

"What is it?"

"I think I might have done something bad. Something terrible."

This got his attention. Jojo sat up and dug through his junk for his SpongeBob shoes. Those were terrible shoes, which upset me even worse.

Jojo crawled out of his hut. He stared up at the stars and said something about "the light of God's love." Then we went for a walk.

I told him what happened with Mugs. Going slowly at first, but then blurting out the rest in a rush of tears.

Jojo put his hand on my shoulder and listened. Just like he always does.

Diego texted me the next morning and told me there was a problem with Strawberry. I had been up late with Jojo, but I felt better now, so I got dressed and went down to the basketball courts.

Jax and Diego were there. Jax said that Strawberry had not been back to the shed. She'd slept in the grass by the chess tables that night, without even a sleeping bag. He was very worried about her. He wanted me to talk to her.

So I went to the Pizza Slice and found her, sitting on the

curb, looking like a leprechaun. She was throwing pieces of pizza crust to the seagulls.

I sat down beside her. I didn't say anything at first. I helped her feed the seagulls.

Finally I said, "Jax said you haven't stayed at that place he found you."

"I don't like it there."

"Why not?"

"It's too far."

"Yeah. It's pretty far."

"And it's dark."

"Maybe we could get you a lamp," I said. "Or a TV."

"I don't like TV," she said.

"Why not?"

"It tells you things that aren't true."

I nodded. She was probably right about that. "Don't you at least want to keep your stuff there?"

"I don't have any stuff."

"What about your backpack?"

She shook her head.

"Okay," I said. I looked at her. "You know, we just worry about you. It's dangerous out here."

"I'm not afraid."

"Okay then," I said.

I got up and walked back to the basketball court. They threw me the ball and waited for me to say something. But there was nothing to say.

TWENTY ONE

The next night, Ailis and I drove to the Topanga trailer park. This was on Jojo's advice.

On the drive, I told Ailis the whole Mugs story: the way Buckalter approached me, the disposable phone, the fact that I never knew where Buckalter was, or who exactly he worked for. And then getting sucker punched on the pier by the old man and his friends.

"And now you're going back?" she said. "To talk to those same people?"

"That's what Jojo said to do. And he's right. I gotta find out what happened. Or at least offer to help if I can."

"You need closure," said Ailis.

"I need to sleep at night," I said.

Ailis pulled into the Topanga parking lot. Her car lights

swept across the old school bus, still packed to the ceiling with crap.

We parked close to the entrance so we could get out fast if we needed to. Ailis shut off the car. We both sat there for a moment. I released my seat belt and opened my door.

Ailis did too.

"What are you doing?" I said.

"I'm coming too, right?"

"Into that thing?" I said, pointing at the decrepit school bus.

"Well, you're going," said Ailis.

"Yeah, but this is my problem," I said. "And things might get weird."

"Then I should be there."

"Yeah, except that you're a girl."

She glared at me. "I'm gonna pretend you didn't say that."

"Ailis, seriously. They might beat the crap out of us," I said.

"Then they beat the crap out of us."

"They might kill us."

"They aren't going to *kill* us," said Ailis. "This is company business. And I'm in the company."

"Listen, we haven't exactly decided about that," I said.

"I thought we *had* decided on that."

"Well, yeah," I said. "We have decided. But we haven't figured out the actual rules of things yet."

"What rules?"

"Like situations like this!" I said, exasperated. "This is dangerous. You have parents. And people who..."

"What?"

"People who would miss you if something happened."

"And you don't?"

"No, I don't. Who's going to miss me? Diego? Strawberry?"

"Yes. Diego and Strawberry. I'm your partner and I'm coming."

"Oh yeah? Well, I *started* this business and if I say it's too dangerous, then you wait here."

"Oh, you started the business? So you decide what I do? Last I heard *partners* means *equal*. And I have *the car*, remember. It's fifteen miles back to Venice from here."

She had me there.

So we both went.

We got out of the car and crept slowly toward the bus. We didn't have a strategy or a backup plan or any weapons to defend ourselves with. We were just going to do this somehow. I replayed my conversation with Jojo in my head. He had promised me this was the best thing to do.

We walked along the side of the school bus, to the folding door in front. It was old and rusty. Ailis and I looked at each other for a moment. I took a deep breath. I knocked softly.

Nothing happened.

I cupped my hands around my face and stared in through

the dirty glass of the door. All I could see was crap. Old paper bags and bottles and plastic crates and a bike tire and a busted birdcage and an old telephone...

I knocked again, harder. Finally a faint light came on somewhere. I heard a voice, then the sharp yap of the tiny dog.

Ailis was being brave, but the dog confused her. "These people have pets?"

"He's got this little dog," I explained.

A figure appeared in the front of the bus. I stepped back. The folding door began to shake. You could hear the rusty mechanism being worked. It finally folded over to the side. In the dim light, several feet above me, I could see the old man, with his white beard and an old baseball hat. A tangy, homeless-person smell wafted out of the bus.

The little dog appeared. He barked and bounded down the steps. He sniffed at us and jumped up against Ailis, his tail wagging wildly. Ailis was good with animals and immediately went into her routine: "*Hey there, little guy! How ya doin', little guy?*"

The old man stared down at me. "So it's you," he said.

"Uh, yeah," I said.

I listened then. I tried to feel the air, to sense if those other guys, the younger guys, might be in the bus too. But there seemed to be no one else present. The old man was alone.

"Who's that?" he said, pointing at Ailis.

"This is Ailis," I said. "She's a...friend."

"Nice to meet you, sir," said Ailis, still playing with the dog. "And who's this?"

"That's Duke," said the old guy.

"*Duuuuuke*," gushed Ailis, patting the dog, which was loving the attention.

Once the formalities were done with, the man focused a tight glare on me.

I tried to remember Jojo's advice.

"Sir," I said, "I wanted to apologize for what happened on the pier. Stomping on your friend's foot. And also for lying to you about Mugs. I told you that I wanted to talk to him about a puppy. But actually someone else was looking for him. And they asked me to help. They paid me."

I was so nervous, I had to stop to catch my breath. Then I continued, "But I was also telling you the truth when I said I didn't know where Mugs was. The guy who hired me didn't tell me who was looking for him. I asked, but he said he didn't know. He thought it was family stuff."

The old man's lower lip began to tremble slightly.

"I feel really bad now," I said, lowering my head. "I think about Mugs all the time. I don't know where he is. I worry about him and I feel responsible for whatever happened to him."

When I looked up, the man's face had turned a deep shade of red. He looked deeply troubled, angry, and confused. He opened his mouth to speak, but he kind of froze up.

And then he collapsed.

He didn't actually fall. He couldn't fall because there was so much crap in there. He leaned backward into a stack of stuff. A shoe box fell and bounced off his shoulder along with a shower of nails and bolts and screws and things.

Ailis was the first to react. She shot up the steps and grabbed him, helping him settle into a sitting position. I followed but it was a tight fit inside that bus, plus he was heavy and old and it was strange to be so close to a man like that. I guess if you had a grandfather you might be used to old people, but I didn't have one, at least none that I knew of. Jojo would have said to treat this man like *he* were my grandfather. So that's what I tried to do.

"Do you have any water?" Ailis asked him as she held him upright.

He didn't answer at first, but after a few seconds, he seemed to regain his senses. He waved his hand toward the back of the bus.

I took that job upon myself. I squeezed through the moldy books, the dishes, the plastic containers, the cardboard boxes. I managed to get into a slightly more open space near the back of the bus. This area was more practically arranged. There were little shelves with cans of food and a small stove/kitchen setup. It was actually pretty similar to my treehouse.

I spotted a plastic gallon jug of drinking water and a coffee cup, and wormed my way back to where Ailis was. In the faint light, I poured the old man some water and held it to his mouth.

"Mr. Torres?" said Ailis loudly. "Can you talk? Do you need us to call an ambulance?"

"I...I'm fine...." he sputtered. He took a tiny sip of the water.

I looked over at Ailis. "Torres?" I said. "Is that his name?"

Ailis pointed at a medical bracelet around his wrist. "Lawrence Torres," she said. "He has diabetes."

I helped him drink more water. "Torres was Mugs's last name," I whispered to Ailis.

"What does that mean?" she whispered back.

"What do you think it means?" rasped the old man. "Mugs is my son."

Eventually, Mr. Torres was able to get to his feet. He assured us he was fine. He wanted to go to Mugs's trailer, to look for clues of what might have happened. "I've been afraid to go in there," he told us. "But since you're here, this must be the time."

He lit an old kerosene lantern, and we helped him down the steps. We walked across the parking lot to Mugs's trailer. Lawrence didn't have a key to the door, but with a couple hard tugs I managed to pop it open. The three of us stepped inside. It was small but clean and livable.

Lawrence set the kerosene lamp on the little table. We all stood there, studying the tiny space.

"The woman who owns this thing hasn't been around for a while," said Lawrence.

Ailis and I were afraid to touch anything. But Lawrence started opening drawers, looking for things.

Under the seat cushions, he found several storage compartments, which he and Ailis dug through.

I started looking around too. One thing about being a foster kid, you got to be a good "hider." That's often the only way you could keep anything for any amount of time. But it also turned you into a good "finder." That was what I did now. I opened some cabinets back by the sleeping area. I checked under the foam mattress. I tried the drawers in the very back of the trailer. One of them felt weirdly heavy. I looked more closely inside it. There were some papers, some old batteries, pieces of a flashlight. But it was heavier than that. I tried to pull the drawer all the way out. There was something blocking it. I emptied it and carefully worked it out of its compartment. Then I turned it over. Under the drawer, duct-taped to the bottom, was a small black pistol.

"Lawrence?" I said.

He came over. "I expected as much," he said. Ailis and I watched while he carefully pulled the tape off the gun. He gripped it, inspected it, and in a quick, fluid motion, swung it toward the window.

Ailis recoiled behind me. I covered my ears. But he didn't pull the trigger. He was just feeling it, testing its weight. He pushed a button and a metal clip dropped out of the handle. He studied this clip. He smelled it. He counted the bullets.

"What can you tell?" I said.

"It's been fired. Three times."

"By Mugs?"

"That would seem likely."

"Maybe he was doing target practice," said Ailis.

"You don't shoot three rounds at target practice," said Lawrence.

We all fell silent.

Lawrence placed the gun on the table. He sat down on the bench seat beside it.

"You kids," he said. "There's something you need to know."

We were all ears.

"Mugs was bad news," he said. "Bad news from the start." He picked up the gun again and looked at it. "I don't know what he did, but whatever it was, he probably did it for the wrong reasons and to the wrong people. And from what you say, it was probably those same people who came looking for him...."

"Don't worry, Mr. Torres," said Ailis. "We'll find out what happened to him. We know people. Cali knows a detective in the police department. We'll find out, right Cali?"

I smiled weakly at her. Lawrence looked away.

"Wait," said Ailis, looking confused. "So we're *not* going to find out?"

"You're never gonna know," said Lawrence, in a low voice. "And the police sure aren't gonna waste their time."

Ailis looked at me. But I lowered my eyes. The old man was right.

For a brief moment, there was no sound except for the hiss of the kerosene lantern burning on the table.

Lawrence spoke in a low voice: "I just hope Mugs finds peace. Wherever he is. He sure never had any on this earth."

Lawrence got to his feet. "Thank you for coming here," he said, making eye contact with both of us. "I appreciate it."

He took the gun and the three of us slowly made our way back to the school bus. At the folding door, he thanked us again.

"Sir?" I said before he disappeared inside. "Can I ask you a favor?"

"What would that be?"

I pointed at the pistol. "Could you maybe sometime... when you're not busy... teach me about guns? I want to be a private investigator."

He stared hard at me for a moment. "Let me tell you something, kid," he said. "No honest man needs a gun. It didn't do Mugs no good. And it won't do you no good, either."

With that, he turned and went into his bus.

TWENTY TWO

I had no bad dreams that night. The next morning, I woke from a deep sleep to the sounds of birds in the trees around me. I rolled over and pushed my door open. The sky was blue. The air smelled like flowers and oranges and the ocean wind. Jojo had been right. I had done the right thing and now I was free again, or as free as I could feel, since I would probably never know what actually happened.

I sat up. I tossed my old Vans into the grass and crawled down my ladder barefoot. I was hoping since it was late morning that Hope would be volunteering at the animal shelter and I'd have the house to myself. I could make some breakfast and blast *Van Halen II*, which I'd recently found at the library.

But Hope wasn't gone; she was in the kitchen. She was

talking to someone, I could hear them laughing. I could smell coffee brewing.

I didn't want to disturb them so I went through to the bathroom and brushed my teeth. Hope called out to me.

"Cali! Come in here. A friend of yours is here!"

I walked into the kitchen, unsure who it could be.

It was Reese Abernathy.

"Hello, Cali," said Reese, smiling at me, her beautiful face glowing with morning freshness.

"Reese didn't want to wake you," said Hope. "So I made some coffee. It turns out she volunteers at the animal shelter too."

"No, I *want* to volunteer," said Reese. "I used to volunteer at a dog shelter at home. It was my favorite extracurricular."

Hope had no idea who Reese was. I hadn't told Hope about my private-investigator business, and Reese was so attractive, and nice, and had such good manners that Hope had done what everyone did with Reese: She had totally fallen for her. She was utterly charmed.

"Uh...hi..." I said to Reese.

"You look sleepy," she said. Then she smiled that smile of hers, and I was, just like Hope, completely under her spell.

Reese wanted to take a drive up the coast. Did I want to come? I did. Hope was late for her shift at the shelter so

Reese offered her a ride. Reese had somehow got a car. The three of us went outside, and Reese beeped the remote of a brand-new Range Rover SUV, with every imaginable luxury you could put in a car. Hope was a pretty down-to-earth person but even she couldn't resist waving to her friends as we rolled up in front of the animal shelter. They were surprised and impressed with the car and with Reese, who waved to them like she was someone famous. She sure looked famous.

With Hope gone, Reese and I continued to the Pacific Coast Highway. I was now in the front seat. She explained that a friend of a friend was letting her use her car and stay at her house. She didn't want to say much else about it. Which made sense. I didn't ask.

We drove north toward Malibu. I amused myself by trying out the different gadgets, moving my seat around, getting a vibrating massage, adjusting a video monitor.

Reese put on some music and I stopped playing with everything. We just rode for a while. It was nice. The ocean, the sky. Reese put her window down. Warm air swirled through the car.

"So where are we going?" I said over the wind.

"I thought we'd go for a picnic," shouted Reese.

"Sounds good," I shouted back.

We drove through Topanga and I pointed out the Topanga Beach parking lot. You could see the school bus from the highway.

"See that old bus?" I yelled.

She looked down into the parking lot. "Yeah?"

"This old guy lives in it," I said. "There's a stove in there and a bed, and he has a dog and everything."

"So he's *off the grid*?" asked Reese. She had liked this expression when I'd used it before.

"Yeah, pretty much."

"So once you go off the grid, can you ever get back on?" asked Reese.

"Sure," I said. "That's what'll happen to me. When I turn eighteen. I'll become a real person again."

"And that'll be good?"

"Sure. I can buy a car. I can sign up for things. I can go to the dentist."

"You can have a real life," said Reese.

The wind was still rushing around. It was blowing Reese's hair into her face. She put up her window, and it was suddenly quiet again. "Have you ever had a girlfriend?" she asked me.

"Me?" I said, embarrassed by the question. "No. Not really."

"You're going to like it," she said. "Having a girlfriend."

"I am?"

"Yeah. It's great."

"You've had boyfriends?" I asked her.

"Of course."

"Like who?"

"Like my tennis instructor."

"Really?" I said.

"*No.*" She grinned at me. "Jeez, Cali. My life isn't a total cliché!"

"Well, how would I know?" I said.

She smiled at how gullible I was.

"So what's so great about having a girlfriend?" I asked.

She shrugged. "Everything," she said. She thought for a second. "Like at first there's the physical stuff. You get super into each other. That's really fun, obviously. And everything she says or does will seem like the most amazing thing ever. And then, as time goes on, you'll get used to each other and the physical stuff will calm down a little. But that's good in a way. You'll start to notice other things. You'll know what her favorite food is. What she thinks about. All her little mannerisms. And what she looks like when she's eating or reading or sleeping."

I nodded along with this. It did sound pretty good.

"And then one day you'll do something together and it won't be fun. The first time that happens it'll scare you, but then you'll see that it's okay. You'll trust each other like that. You can be bored together. You can have a crappy day. You can have any kind of day. It won't change things."

She signaled and changed lanes. "And then even worse things will happen," she continued. "One of you will fart. Or do something really stupid or embarrassing. And you'll be like, oh my god, she couldn't possibly still like me after I did that. But that won't matter, either, not in the end. And then eventually, gradually, you'll come to know each other completely. Like all the way through. From head to toe. And that's love, I guess. I think it is. I mean, other people have different ideas. But to me, that's love. That's your first boyfriend. Or girlfriend. That's the first one that really counts."

I sat thinking about this. I had never heard relationships described like this before. But that was Reese. She made everything seem totally new and different and like you'd never even thought about it before.

"Has that stuff happened to you?" I finally asked.

"Parts of it have. Some parts. But all of it, start to finish? No."

"None of it's happened to me," I said. "That's for sure."

She smiled over at me. "Well, you have something to look forward to then, don't you?"

We passed through Malibu and drove farther, passed Zuma Beach, and then beyond anywhere I had ever been before. There were no more houses, no more buildings. It was just brown desert hills and the highway curving around the rocky seashore. And the ocean, of course, with its perfect flatness, perfect blueness, sparkling in the sunshine.

Reese pulled over at an unmarked spot. Stashed in the back, she had an actual picnic basket and a big tote bag. She gave me the heavy stuff to carry and we crawled down through the rocks to a secluded beach she somehow knew about.

We got settled on the beach. I found myself talking about Ailis. "I have this friend. She's a girl. I think we're going to start a business together."

"What sort of business?" Reese asked, moving behind some rocks to change into her swimsuit.

"Private investigating," I said. "Finding people. Like what I do now, but on my own. And with Ailis..."

"That sounds like a great idea," said Reese from behind her rock.

"Do you really think so?"

"Of course," she said. "You can use your own life experience."

"The finding-people part I'm not worried about," I said. "I just don't know about the business part. I've never even had a job...."

"My dad always says you should work for yourself. And I'm sure you can figure it out. Is Ailis smart? Can she help you?"

"Yeah, she's great. I mean, we argue sometimes...you know...but she has good ideas."

Reese detected something in my tone.

"Do you like her, this girl?"

"Ailis? No. Not at all. She's...I mean...no. I don't like her. Not like that."

Reese watched me closely.

"I don't. Really. I don't."

* ❁ * ❁ * ❁ *

We spread out our towels. Reese lay on her stomach, reading a magazine. I found the food in the picnic basket, all of which was super fancy: grapes and olives and crumbly goat cheese and this delicious bread, which had a lot of holes in it.

Reese started telling me about her week, how she'd had some close calls with some of the men her father had hired. One guy had followed her into American Apparel in Beverly Hills and she'd had to convince the girls who worked there that she was being stalked so they'd let her out the secret "stalker" exit. At other times, she'd worn a wig and changed her whole look. "You're not going to tell on me, are you?" she said.

"No," I said.

She flipped through her magazine. "My dad even came down here. To check on the progress for himself."

I hadn't mentioned seeing her dad yet. But now I had to. "Yeah, actually, I saw him."

She turned and blinked at me. "You saw my dad?"

"He was waiting for me outside Hope's."

Reese dropped her magazine and stared at me. "Are you serious? What did he say?"

"He said..." I didn't want to tell her, but there seemed no way to avoid it. "He said that you sometimes had trouble knowing what was real and what wasn't. That you made stuff up."

181

Reese sat up and frowned into the ocean. "That's what he tells everyone."

"He wanted me back on the case," I said.

"What did you say?"

"I said I would help you if I could, but I wouldn't take any money. And I wouldn't report to him."

"Well, thanks for that anyway," said Reese.

The tide was rising, which was gradually making our little private beach smaller. Waves came in and spread themselves on the sand in front of us.

"So it's not true?" I said. "You don't make stuff up?"

"Well, I'm not crazy! Not like he says," she said. "But I mean, how do you even know? I've had periods where things felt...disconnected. Who hasn't?"

She pushed some sand around. I stared blankly at her smooth, tanned legs.

I said, "Do you know for sure that he killed your mom?"

She thought about that for a long time. She stared into the ocean. "I thought I did. Now I don't know."

"You seemed pretty sure before."

"I was upset," she said. "The truth is, I didn't want to admit that my mother would do that. That she could be so unhappy. Because that meant I would never get better, either. Because I'm so much like her. We were so much alike it's scary."

"Huh," I said.

"That's why I wanted to see you again."

"Me?" I said.

"Because even if my dad didn't kill her, he's still a bad person. I still can't live with him. He hurts people. He *likes* hurting people. My mom said something about divorce once and he told her he would ruin her and make her a bag lady on the street. No offense," she added quickly, "to people who live on the street."

"No offense taken."

"And he lies to everyone," she continued. "He was lying to you when he told you I was lying. That's how he operates. He hits you from every side until you give him what he wants. And if you resist, or fight back, he destroys you. I could never live in the same house with him. Something terrible would happen."

I watched her worried face. It was still beautiful, even when she was dealing with terrible things.

"That's why I wanted to talk to you," she said quietly. "I want to run away. Like really run away. Like away from California. Somewhere he can't find me. Off the grid. Someplace I can start over." She paused for a moment, and raised her eyes to me.

"I want to be like you, Cali," she said. "I want to disappear."

TWENTY THREE

Reese still wanted to see my treehouse, so we went there after the beach.

We parked several blocks from Hope's, in case anyone was watching the house. It was dark now, so that helped. We cut through the alley and crawled over Hope's neighbor's metal fence and then climbed the wood fence to Hope's. Reese was not the greatest fence climber but she was determined, even after she skinned her hand, and got her pant leg caught.

When we were safely in Hope's backyard, I led Reese to the treehouse. She seemed impressed. I went up first and turned on the light so she could see.

"Okay," I said. "Come on up."

She climbed the ladder. She got to the top and I helped

her in. I was suddenly embarrassed, though, as it occurred to me that she probably lived in mansions her whole life, while I lived in a box made of scrap wood, in someone else's backyard.

But she was having so much fun, it made me forget about that. She crawled around and looked at the sleeping area and the little shelves with the radio and my notebooks. I'd stuck some drawings to the wall, including my ideas for the name of our business: MISSING PERSONS INCORPORATED, or MPI for short, and a logo I'd been working on.

I lit some candles to get more light, and pulled in my bag of oranges and offered her one.

"Oh my God," said Reese. "You keep your food outside, hanging from a branch!"

"Just the oranges," I said.

So then, since she liked it so much, I opened up the top hatch and we crawled onto the roof and lay down, face up, like I did with Ailis that time. We stared up at the black sky above us and the passing planes and the glow of downtown Los Angeles to the east.

Reese loved it. She started talking about wanting to be on the road, traveling across the desert, away from her dad and California and all the superficial crap she had known all her life. She didn't need money. She didn't need credit cards or Range Rover SUVs. She wanted to throw herself into the world and see what happened. To live by her wits. To struggle and suffer and find her own way.

I found myself getting swept up in her vision and wishing I could go with her, wherever she was going, and I remembered what her dad said, about how "dreamer" partners are the best. If you have someone like that by your side, you feel like anything is possible.

When we crawled back inside, I waited for her to say she had to leave. But she didn't. So I set up the little hot plate and made us both hot chocolate. We sat and drank it in the candlelight. By now it was pretty late and she smiled at me and said, "Has anyone ever slept up here with you?"

"Uh..." I said, trying to think of a way to explain about Ailis and her abusive dad and the time she freaked out.

"Ailis tried to," I said. "Once."

"Can I sleep here? Tonight?"

My body froze up for a second. I said, "Are you sure you want to?"

"Are you serious?" she said. "Of course I want to. We can spoon!"

I had heard of spooning, but I wasn't sure what it was exactly. But whatever it was, I'd be doing it with Reese. So how bad could it be?

So that's what we did. We sat up and arranged the pad and the blankets and the sleeping bag. Then we took off our shoes and turned off the lights and there we were, under the covers, which was kind of like dying and going to heaven for me, mainly because Reese smelled so good, and her skin was so nice to be next to. Also she was giggling and excited by the whole thing: sleeping in a treehouse, feeling the tree sway and the wind rustle the leaves around us.

Then a cat got on the roof, which happened sometimes. Usually it was Nibbles, the neighbor's cat. Reese didn't know what it was and got scared for a minute, but I told her it was okay, it was just Nibbles, from next door.

She thought that was funny. She said, "Nibbles."

And I said, "Nibbles."

And she started laughing.

And I started laughing.

"Nibbles the Cat..." she said one last time, and I could feel her warm breath on me and it felt so good to be there, so close to her face and her eyes.

Eventually, we stopped talking and she turned her back to me and we "spooned," not with my arms completely around her or anything, but just fitting together like spoons do.

I woke up early. Much earlier than normal. Reese was still asleep. I realized my left hand had somehow ended up completely around her waist. And my chest was snug up against her back. No wonder everyone talks about spooning. It's the best thing in the world.

I closed my eyes again, but there was no way I was going back to sleep. So I lay there, in the early dawn light, with the first birds chirping and the tree silent and still. I moved my face slightly closer to her, so I could breathe her hair and smell her and feel her softness. I got the idea then, that if I concentrated and held her just right, I could meld a part of myself into her. She had such a tough road ahead, maybe I could transfer some of that *survivor* part of me into her. And then if she got into a tight spot, it would be there and it would help her.

Eventually, she woke up. I pretended that I'd been asleep the whole time. We both got up and put our shoes and hoodies back on and climbed down from the treehouse. She yawned and stretched in the yard, and I worried she hadn't slept so well. "You okay?" I asked.

"I'm great!" said Reese, grinning. "That was *soo* fun. Thank you." She took my hand and pulled me to her and kissed me shyly on the cheek.

When she let go, she was blushing and she immediately bent down to retie her shoe. I blushed too and fiddled with my hoodie zipper. That was when I noticed that Hope's back door was open. Someone was standing in the doorway, watching the two of us there in the backyard, having just climbed out of the treehouse where we'd obviously spent the night.

It was Ailis.

Reese left soon after that. Ailis did not. She was there to have breakfast with Hope, at one of Hope's big communal breakfasts. We both joined Hope's friends at the big table. Ailis didn't eat. Mostly she sat across from me, holding a cup of coffee and staring at me with laser death eyes.

Finally, she asked if we could talk. We went outside and stood in front of the house. "Can you please explain what I just saw?" said Ailis, her arms crossed over her chest.

"Reese wanted to see the treehouse."

"And?"

"And it was late. She wanted to see what it was like to sleep there."

"And that seemed like a good idea to you?" Ailis said, staring at me with double-strength laser death eyes.

"What?" I said. "You slept up there."

"Yeah, except there's a couple small differences between me and her," she said. "For starters, I am not one of the people you were hired to find. Second, I am not on Amber Alert across the entire United States. And thirdly I am not...I am not..." She was really getting mad now. "I don't look like that!"

Ailis started to hyperventilate. "Did it ever occur to you that this is the kind of thing that breaks up businesses?" she said. "That you are jeopardizing everything we've worked for?"

"Why would this break up our business?" I asked.

"Because you're not treating it like a business! You're not treating me like a partner. You're doing whatever you feel like. You're not being responsible!"

Ailis began to pace back and forth on the sidewalk. Then

she plopped down on the step. She made a fist with her hand and bounced it against her forehead.

"I'm sorry," I said. "I didn't think about it that way."

Ailis didn't respond. But slowly, she began to breathe normally again. She calmed down.

"Do you like her?" she finally asked me.

Now she was back to being Ailis my friend. She just wanted to know what was going on.

"Yeah, I like her," I said, kicking at a rock on the sidewalk. "She's not like anyone I've ever known before."

"Are you in love with her?"

"What?"

"You heard what I said."

I kicked some more rocks. "I don't know," I told her. This was the honest truth and Ailis could see that it was. "How do you know if you're in love with someone?" I asked.

"I don't know," she said. "I've never been."

"Me neither," I said.

We didn't speak for a while. We both felt ridiculous, I guess, and like we'd revealed more about ourselves than we wanted to.

Then Ailis became agitated again. "Oh my god, I can't believe I yelled at you like that," she said. "I sound like some stupid jealous girlfriend."

I shrugged. "It's okay."

She covered her face with her hands. "It was just the

shock of it," she said. "That's all. What you do on your time has nothing to do with me."

"Hey," I said. "We're friends too. I understand." I jammed my hands into my hoodie pockets. Ailis looked miserable. And tired. I noticed then that her hair was dirty, like she hadn't had a shower in several days.

Which meant her dad was home again. Which explained why she'd shown up at Hope's for breakfast. She'd probably been sleeping in her mom's car.

TWENTY FOUR

MMMMM—Kucha—MMMMM—Kucha—MMMMM—Kucha rolled the wheels of my skateboard on the sidewalk. I turned a wide, slow right and hit the boardwalk, weaving through a group of old-people tourists. A layer of fog was creeping in off the ocean and the sand was damp and the water had that smooth glassiness it gets sometimes, when it looks like a silvery metallic ocean on an alien planet.

I hopped off my board and walked onto the knoll to get a better view of the water. There were surfers beyond the breakers, sitting on their boards, staring out to sea. A large, growing wave appeared and several of the group came to life, turning in place and paddling furiously, in hopes of catching it.

I wanted to be out there. I thought about how simple my

life had been just two months ago. And how complicated it had become. Which was the better way to live? Working hard, going to school, dealing with complicated people and difficult situations? Or living like I had before. No classes. No job. Surfing. Hoops. Eating oranges and day-old veggie burgers from the Dumpster behind Greens-N-Things?

Which was better? I couldn't say. Maybe a little of both.

I went to the basketball courts and played in a game with two guys from Brazil who couldn't speak English. They weren't the best basketball players, but at one point they started kicking the ball around and they were really good at that.

Then Diego showed up on his tiny BMX bike and we got a real game going. Diego and I were on the same team and we were tearing it up, doing our special moves, communicating with our eyes, just a look between us, and a cut to the basket and the bounce pass for the layup.

Later, Jax came by and we cruised to the Pizza Slice to say hi to Strawberry but she wasn't in her normal place on the curb. That was unusual, so we asked Dimitri, the guy who runs the Pizza Slice, where she was. He didn't know. Then Diego got a call from his cousin and we all went to help push somebody's car to the mechanic.

Strawberry still wasn't around that night and Jax came to the basketball court to ask if anyone had seen her. We walked over to the Pizza Slice and asked Dimitri again, but he didn't know where she was, and he didn't like being bothered about it. He never liked us street kids hanging around. But his wife had been orphaned in her home country, in a war, so she was the one who made him be nice to us.

Jax was still worried. So we looked around. I checked the rusty oil drum where Strawbs stashed her backpack. It was still there. So wherever she went, she was planning on coming back.

Jax wanted to look inside the backpack, so I lifted it out of the oil drum. We opened it up. There was a dirty T-shirt, a sweater, a pair of socks, a little plastic thing for her toothbrush, and dental floss. There was an old, beat-up copy of the book *Winnie the Pooh* that had come from a public library in Louisiana. At the very bottom were some coins and a couple of mangled bills, one of which was a twenty, possibly the one I gave her weeks ago. I checked the other pockets of the backpack. There was nothing there of any help. No phone. No ID. Nothing with her name on it. One thing Strawberry knew how to do: not exist.

"How long has it been since you saw her?" I said, lowering her stuff back into the oil drum.

"Two days," said Jax, a look of worry on his face.

"Two days?" I said back.

That was a long time.

Ailis, meanwhile, was working on a website for our business and that night I went over to her house to look at it. Her dad was gone but her mom was there, camped out in front of the

TV with a cocktail in her hand. She got right up, though. You could tell Ailis had told her about me and she wanted to see what my deal was. She chatted me up, asking me questions, where I lived, where I was from. I was polite but avoided saying too much. I told her I was from the Midwest. She said, "Yeah, I can tell."

Ailis waved away her mother and we went into her room. She showed me the website on her computer. MISSING PERSONS INCORPORATED was the name of it. She'd come up with some logo ideas, blowing up the letters M for "Missing" and P for "Persons" and fusing them together. It looked pretty professional. But I wasn't sure we could put this on the Internet without getting into trouble. We didn't have a license. We weren't registered anywhere. I was technically a missing person myself, in the eyes of the Nebraska juvenile courts. So who knew what would happen.

I was shooting baskets the next morning when my phone rang. I checked the number: RESTRICTED.

I took it. It was Reese. The minute I heard her voice, my chest filled with a hollow ache.

She was leaving, she told me. For good. She wanted to meet up before she left. I said sure, though I knew any contact was going to be painful. It wasn't necessarily fun to hang out with people you were in love with, I was learning. Especially if it was to say good-bye.

We agreed to meet at the Milk Bar Cafe on Washington.

I took extreme evasive action getting there—climbing over fences, slipping through alleys—in case Grisham's guys were around, or even Mr. Abernathy himself.

At the Milk Bar, I got a latte and stayed in a corner by the window. I didn't know if Reese was going to be driving the fancy car. Or taking a taxi. But no, she appeared on the street, on foot, with a big REI backpack and her hair tucked under a baseball cap.

She looked excited, and a little scared. She'd bought a Greyhound bus ticket to somewhere back east—she wouldn't tell me. One thing, though: Her backpack was huge and it was stuffed to the brim. It was as heavy as a load of bricks.

"Uh, Reese?" I said, lifting it. "This isn't good."

So then we spent a few minutes in an alley behind the Milk Bar going through her stuff. I explained that you had to be brutal when it came to packing. You had to dump anything that was not absolutely necessary. Like the big bag of hair products she had. Or the two pairs of jeans. Or the six paperback books. "One book at a time," I told her. "You finish one, you trade it for another."

"Who do I trade with?"

"The other people."

"What other people?"

I smiled at her. "All the nice people you're going to meet in the truck stops and bus stations across the country."

When we'd cut her possessions by half, we repacked her

bag. It was a lot lighter. "The trick is," I told her, "less stuff, more money."

A hint of worry flashed across her face.

"What?" I said. "You have money, right?"

"Yeah," she said, hesitating. "Of course."

"How much do you have?"

She seemed reluctant to say.

"C'mon, let's see," I said.

She got out her wallet. We both looked inside.

She had fifty-eight dollars and some change.

"Oh no," I said. "That's not enough. Not even close."

"I can't get any more," she said, embarrassed. "My dad froze my accounts."

"You don't have any cash anywhere?"

She shook her head. "Can't I just do what you do?" she asked. "Find free food? Dumpster dive?"

"Not in the normal world. People will see you. You'll get picked up by the cops."

I looked around. There happened to be a branch of my bank across the street. I looked at it. I looked at Reese.

"Come on," I said, taking her hand.

After that, we went to the pier and sat on a bench facing the ocean. Somewhere out there was Japan and China and other places I didn't know the names of.

It was hard to picture Reese alone in the world. It wasn't

like she wouldn't figure things out. She would. And it wasn't like she could stay here any longer. It was a miracle she hadn't been found already.

Eventually, we walked back to the metro bus stop, which would take her to the Greyhound station downtown. We sat on the bench together. I wanted to tell her stuff, and I did, little tricks of traveling that occurred to me as we sat there. Mostly I told her every way I could think of to stay safe. She listened to me, but we both knew nothing I said was going to make much difference. She'd find her way, like people do.

When I saw the bus coming, my whole body tightened up. We both stood up. And then I couldn't restrain myself anymore. I threw my arms around her. I held her to me as tightly as I could. Tears came into my eyes. She hugged me back, and then gently pulled away. I could see she was crying too, a little, but also smiling.

The bus hissed to a stop. I helped her lift her backpack onto her shoulder.

The doors opened. Reese turned to me. "Do you know what Strawberry told me, the day I met her on the boardwalk?"

"What?"

"She said you were the prince of Venice Beach."

"What does that mean?"

"It means you're a good person. And that your friends love you."

I took in that information. I didn't know what to do with it.

"You comin' or not?" said the driver.

Reese leaned forward and kissed me on the lips: a single, precious, unhurried kiss.

"Let's go!" repeated the driver.

Reese steadied herself and then climbed onto the bus. The doors immediately closed behind her.

I stepped backward and watched the bus go. The ache in my chest was so deep and painful I had to sit back down on the bench. I lowered my head, so people wouldn't see the tears falling between my shoes.

TWENTY FIVE

For the next couple days, I fell back into my old routine.
Hoops in the morning. Surf in the afternoon. I couldn't think
of what else to do with myself.

Jax and I kept checking back at the Pizza Slice for any
signs of Strawberry. It had been several more days since anyone had seen her. Jax was getting a little desperate now. One
night, when Dimitri said something to us about moving away
from the Pizza Slice window if we weren't going to buy anything, Jax started yelling at him through the little window.
Jax kind of lost it. This was not good, as Dimitri was someone we all relied on pretty heavily for the occasional free slice
or odd job. Dimitri threatened to call the cops and I had to
drag Jax away from the Pizza Slice.

The next morning, first thing, I swung by the Pizza Slice again. There was still no sign of Strawberry. I did a full boardwalk cruise that morning. I started asking around. But nobody knew anything. Nobody had seen her or knew where she was.

That afternoon I played basketball with Diego and some of his cousins. But everyone seemed in a bad mood. People were pushing. Elbows were flying.

Then Jax showed up. He wanted me to come to the police station with him, to see if they knew anything. So we went.

Jax didn't like being in the police station. I wasn't so happy about it, either. At the desk, I asked to see Darius Howard, but he wasn't there. So we talked to a lady cop instead. She listened to our story. Then she checked her computer. They hadn't picked up anybody fitting Strawberry's description. Nor had anybody died who might have been her. Since we didn't know her real name or address, there wasn't much else they could do.

Afterward, we walked down to the pier. I tried to remind Jax as delicately as I could that Strawberry had appeared out of nowhere, and might disappear the same way. But he didn't want to hear that.

Later, we stopped by the Pizza Slice again. I kept Jax away from Dimitri and talked to him myself. Dimitri wasn't pissed now. He was worried about Strawbs just like we were. I watched him for a moment, with his dirty apron, stuck in his tiny kitchen making pizzas all day. It wasn't like his life was so great.

Then, as we passed Café Italia, Jax suddenly stopped and pulled me into a doorway. "Look who it is," he whispered.

I looked. Sitting at one of the outside tables were the Evil Twins.

"What?" I said.

"It's those guys."

"What about them?" I said.

"They might know where Strawberry is."

I hadn't thought of that. The Evil Twins probably knew more about what happened in Venice than anyone. Especially the sketchy stuff.

"Dude, I'm not talking to them," I said. "They beat the crap out of me and stole my skateboard!"

"Dude," said Jax. "Strawbs has been gone for a week. I don't care if they killed their own mothers. We gotta find out if they know anything."

So we approached the café patio, moving slowly, carefully. As we got closer, I got a good daylight look at the twins. They looked even more evil than usual.

We arrived at their table. I let Jax start the conversation.

"Hey," said Jax, his voice faltering slightly.

They glared at us with cold, threatening stares. If they remembered robbing me, they didn't show it.

"Can we...uh...talk to you guys for a second?" said Jax.

They barely acknowledged us. "What about?" said the blond twin.

"We need help," said Jax.

"We don't help people," said the dark-haired twin.

"We need your advice," I said. "We need your knowledge of the boardwalk."

The blond twin stirred his coffee. Jax gestured for me to get my phone out, since I had a picture of Strawbs on it.

"It's about our friend Strawberry," said Jax. "She's missing."

Jax cautiously took a seat at the table and tried to show the blond twin my phone picture of Strawbs.

He barely glanced at it. "What is she, some runaway chick?" he said. "So she left. So what? That's what runaways do. They *run away*."

"She didn't take her stuff, though," said Jax.

"So maybe she left in a hurry."

"It's weird that she wouldn't say anything," I said. "We were buddies."

"Buddies?" scoffed the dark-haired twin, bored, looking at the phone. But then he looked closer. He recognized her. "Oh yeah," he said. "The chick with the pizza sign."

"Exactly," said Jax. "Her name is Strawberry."

"That's a stupid name," said the blond twin. "What is it with these girls named after flavors? Pretty soon there's gonna be chicks named Grape. Or Butterscotch."

The two of them smiled at that. I saw the dark-haired one was still wearing Chad Mitchell's thick gold watch. Which bugged me.

"Could you maybe ask around?" said Jax. "You guys know a lot of people."

The blond twin glared at us. "What's that supposed to mean?"

"Nothing," I said, speaking up. "Just that you guys have more connections than us. You could put out the word."

"We don't do people favors."

"Well, maybe we could do something for you," said Jax.

"What could you possibly do for us?" said the dark-haired twin, staring hard at both of us.

Jax and I tried to think of something.

"Just like I thought," he said. "You got nothin'."

"How about money," said the blond twin. "You got any of that?"

That was a painful question for me. I *had* money. But I'd just given it all to Reese.

"I didn't think so," he grumbled.

Then, as if to humiliate us further, the blond twin looked again at the photo. He took the phone from my hands and studied it closely. "I know this girl. Strawberry is her name? Ha-ha. Figures."

"You know her?" said Jax. "When did you see her last?"

The blond twin shrugged. "I saw her...a day ago? Or maybe it was a week ago. I dunno. I lose track of time sometimes. Maybe if I had some more coffee..."

He looked at Jax sideways. Jax grabbed his wallet out of his pocket. "I'll buy you a coffee."

"I think I need two coffees. Actually, I think I need about three hundred bucks."

"Dude, I don't got three hundred bucks," said Jax.

"Of course you don't have three hundred bucks, you *frickin' street scum*. How would *you* get three hundred bucks?"

Jax didn't answer.

The blond twin looked back at the phone. His voice softened: "Now little Strawberry here, *she* might be worth three hundred bucks...."

Jax's face started to burn. I saw the muscles flex in his jaw.

"A young girl like this..." the blond twin said. "Clean her up a bit.... Now you've got something a person might be willing to pay for...."

I could feel that Jax was about to explode. I casually took the phone back from the blond twin, pretending to look at the picture again, I slyly texted Diego: *Café Italia. Need backup.*

Then the phone was grabbed out of my hands. "What are you doing with my phone?" said the blond twin.

"Uh...that's my phone," I corrected him.

"I don't think so," said the blond twin. "This is *my* phone. And you just tried to take it from me."

"You guys might want to think about moving on," said the dark-haired twin. "The management here doesn't like beggars in their café."

"We're not *begging*," I said.

"*No, I don't have a dollar!*" said the blond twin loudly, in the direction of one of the waiters. As he did this, he slipped my phone into his pocket.

The waiter came toward Jax and me, as if to shoo us away. Another café employee, maybe a manager, appeared at the door and also moved in our direction.

"I want my phone back," I said quietly to the blond twin, though there was no way I could make him do it.

Jax snapped. He grabbed the glass sugar jar from the middle of the table and slammed the butt of it into the middle of the dark-haired twin's face. You could hear his nose break. The blond twin, quick as a cat, lunged forward, grabbed Jax by the front of his shirt, and dragged him over the table and onto the floor. I grabbed at the blond twin, but he was too big and too strong. Plus the waiter had joined in. He grabbed Jax too and helped the blond twin force him to the ground.

Meanwhile, the dark-haired twin, with his face bleeding, struggled to his feet and then attacked Jax, viciously kicking and punching him. All three of them began raining blows down on him.

I did the only thing I could do. I picked up Jax's chair and swung it down as hard as I could on the top of the dark-haired twin's head. This knocked him down, but then the blond twin picked up *his* chair and swung it at me, very nearly chopping my head off with it.

I don't know what happened after that exactly. I got tackled by a different person and was wrestled to the ground. Suddenly several large bodies were on top of me with someone's forearm on my neck, pressing down and making it impossible to breathe.

Then, at the last possible moment, a wavelike *surge* seemed to enter the patio, rearranging everything in its path. The people on top of me were suddenly torn loose. Tables turned over. Tourists scattered. Coffee cups, dishes, umbrellas crashed to the ground.

This was Diego and six of his cousins. The waiter, who had been the one choking me, was thrown into a table, all his tips and change spraying out of his apron onto the ground. Diego got the blond twin in a headlock and rode him face-first into the concrete, landing his full 235 pounds on the twin's cranium. The manager, on his hands and knees, crawled pathetically toward the kitchen. He got dragged back into the fight by his ankles.

And then the cop cars pulled up, several of them, lights flashing, sirens squawking. I studied the scene from under a table. There was no escape. We were all trapped in the front of the café, mostly by the huge crowd of tourists who had gathered to watch the patio-clearing brawl. Then, to my right, I saw the dark-haired twin, facedown among the broken glass, groaning and trying to stand.

I crept over to him and stomped my foot down on his elbow, pinning it to the ground. As he gasped with pain, I reached down and tore Chad Mitchell's thick gold watch off his wrist.

Which I found out later was made in China and didn't even work.

TWENTY SIX

I thought about Nebraska as I sat in the large empty holding cell in the Santa Monica Juvenile Detention Center. What would it be like to be back there?

They'd send me on a bus probably, handcuffed to the seat in front of me. My return would be my original trip in reverse. The same highways. The same Burger Kings along the interstate. And then I'd be back in Omaha, back in the Nebraska system. I'd get transferred around to the different facilities. Maybe I'd remember some of the people. Maybe they'd put me with my old foster-care counselor. She'd be like, "Where have you been?" And I'd say, "You wouldn't believe me if I told you."

It was about ten thirty at night when I heard my cell being

unlocked. A guard came in and handcuffed me. In my paper slippers and orange jumpsuit, I was led down the clean white hallway into an empty visitors area. Apparently there weren't a lot of juvenile offenders in Santa Monica.

There, I was surprised to see Ailis's smiling face through the Plexiglas. She wasn't really smiling, I saw. She was trying to smile.

I took a seat, my hands cuffed together in front of me. "Hey," I said.

"Oh, Cali," said Ailis, sadly, as she looked at me.

"Do I look that bad?" I asked.

"No, no," she assured me. "It's just the jumpsuit...." Ailis had to take a breath to calm herself.

"Where's Jax and Diego?" I asked.

She lowered her voice. "I think Diego got away. They got Jax, though. And those other guys."

"What about me? Are they gonna let me out?"

"I don't know," said Ailis. "They said they have to process you, and then tomorrow you'll go before the judge."

"They're gonna send me back to Nebraska," I said.

"One of the people said..." Ailis swallowed hard. "If it's felony assault...you could go to the state penitentiary."

"Great."

Ailis was doing her best to remain upbeat and positive. "I'm going to talk to Hope about it. She's been very helpful. She knows a lawyer who helps poor people."

"Okay."

"There's another thing," she said. "They found Strawberry."

I braced myself for the worst.

"She's been living in the storage room at the animal shelter. They're letting her volunteer there. And she was sneaking in the back after hours."

I almost laughed with relief.

"The people there think she's weird," continued Ailis. "But I guess the animals like her."

"You gotta tell Jax. Do you know where he is? He wasn't in the holding cell—"

But just then a door opened behind Ailis. A cop in full uniform appeared. Then another. Behind them, a tall, serious black man in a suit coat hurried forward. He was wearing glasses. It was the glasses I recognized first. And then the face underneath them.

It was Darius Howard.

"Hey, kid," he said.

"Detective Howard!" I said.

Ailis, too, was surprised to hear his name.

A plainclothes cop who was also with Detective Howard went immediately to the side door that separated my area from Ailis's. He unlocked it. He gestured to the guard standing over me, who immediately undid my handcuffs.

"I got a situation, Robert," said Darius. "I need your help."

I was led through to the other room. Some more police had appeared. A woman cop handed me my clothes, my wallet, and Chad Mitchell's gold watch.

The half-dozen adults and Ailis stood watching while the woman cop helped me change out of the jumpsuit.

"Is he free?" said Ailis.

"For now," said Darius, who was watching his phone. The other men with him were also watching their phones. Or talking urgently into them.

"What is it?" I said.

"Can't say. It's sensitive. But we gotta move."

"Wait, you're taking him somewhere?" said Ailis.

"Just for now. We need him. It's police business."

Ailis's mind began to work. "Well, if you want his help, you have to drop the assault charges," she said.

Darius Howard looked at his phone. "That's a separate issue."

"No, it isn't," said Ailis, emphatically. "If he's gonna help you, you have to help him."

Darius Howard held up a finger and turned away from Ailis. He was taking a call. "Yes, sir," he said into his phone. "I know, sir. Tell the governor we'll be there in thirty minutes."

He ended the call and slipped the phone into his jacket pocket. "Come on, Robert," he said.

But Ailis jumped in front of me. "No! He's not going any-where until you agree to drop the charges. He didn't start that fight. He was trying to help his friend."

Darius considered Ailis for the first time. "Who are you?"

"I'm Ailis. I'm Cali's partner."

"We don't have time for this," someone said to Darius. "We need to go."

"All right," said Darius, waving me forward. "All charges are dropped."

And with that, Darius, myself, and two of the plain-clothes cops left the room and began running down the hall.

We ran up four flights of metal stairs and onto the roof of the detention center, where a police helicopter had just set down. Needless to say, I'd never been around a real helicop-ter before. It was very loud and powerful. You could barely run toward it. But we did, Darius and then me and then two other men in suits.

We'd barely strapped in when we lifted off the building and banked wildly to the right. My stomach felt like it might fall out through my feet. We accelerated upward and in a few seconds I could see all of Santa Monica and Venice and the dark ocean spread out before us. The chopper leaned far for-ward and began to speed up the coast toward Malibu.

We flew up the coast for about ten minutes and then descended at a gut-dropping speed, landing in a gravel park-ing lot near the beach. There we unbuckled ourselves and ran through the noise and the dust to an unmarked police car that immediately took off down the highway at about ninety miles an hour. The trip had been so noisy and chaotic I hadn't even had a chance to speak with Darius. Now I leaned forward and tried to ask him what was happening. But he was on his phone again.

A moment later, the car turned into a gated entrance. Two men in suits and headsets stood on either side of it.

My heart began to pound. What was happening? And why did they need me?

We sped down a private driveway and approached one of the largest mansions I had ever seen. There was a squad car and several other unmarked police cars in the circular driveway in front. There was also an ambulance and a black Suburban with tinted windows and government plates. Two men stood beside it like bodyguards.

What on earth was this?

Our car skidded to a stop. Darius and I jumped out of the car and were guided in through the front door.

The inside of the house was mostly dark. People had small, pen-shaped flashlights to guide us along a hallway and then down a wide stairwell. In front of the stairs was a huge plate-glass window that looked over the backyard and out to the ocean. I heard someone behind me whisper into a headset, "Darius is here. With the kid..."

We continued down the stairs and then came to a back door, which was guarded by two more men. One of them walked with us into the backyard, stealthily guiding us across a wide patio, around a swimming pool, and into a large pool house.

All of this was in the dark. No one else was in the back-yard. It was so quiet and still out there I could hear the lapping of the pool water as it bumped against the tiles.

Darius and I entered the pool house. Inside were four men in suits as well as several men with weapons and full SWAT gear. One of them was holding a tranquilizer dart as I stepped around him. No overhead lights were on, but you could see from the glow of people's phones and the tiny flash-lights. Along the back wall was a large window, where most of the people were gathered. From the window, I finally saw what the focus of all this attention was: a small one-room building—an art studio, someone said—sat just downhill from us. It was at the edge of the lawn, very near the cliff that I assumed dropped down to the ocean. It had no lights on inside. The drapes were closed. It looked empty.

Darius Howard, beside me, stared at it through the window and took a long breath.

"Any movement?" he asked the other men.

"No, sir."

"Any phone contact?"

"Not a word."

Across the room, I spotted another familiar figure in

the dim light. I couldn't see him clearly, but I recognized his shape, and then his voice when he began arguing frantically with one of the plainclothes cops.

"Mr. Abernathy," said the cop. "Please. Keep your voice down!"

TWENTY SEVEN

Darius explained the situation: Reese was in the studio. She had a gun. She had fired a single round at the house, earlier in the evening, when the first police officers had arrived.

"She's off her medication," Darius Howard said in his low, steady voice. "And it's not a pretty picture."

"A psychotic breakdown," said someone else. "She could do anything in her present state."

Mr. Abernathy remained agitated on his side of the room. There was a hushed argument going on. Again, someone told him to be quiet.

"*You* be quiet!" he hissed. "That's my daughter out there!"

Darius Howard pulled me closer to the window, away from Mr. Abernathy.

"We had her on the phone earlier," he said quietly. "The line is still open but she's not speaking to us. We need you to talk to her. We need you to get her outta there. Without the gun."

I nodded that I understood. But really I was confused. Reese was in that little house? How had that happened? She was supposed to be back east by now. And where did she get a gun? And whose mansion was this?

"Gimme the phone," said Darius to one of his men. The phone was passed forward. It was patched into a small speaker so everyone could hear.

Darius handed it to me. I reluctantly put it to my ear. Through the glass, I watched the darkened studio. It showed no signs of life.

"Hello?" I said into the phone.

No answer.

"Reese?" I said. "This is Cali. Are you there?"

I looked around at the grim adult faces staring at me. A full five seconds passed.

Then a sound...a bump...A female voice said, "Cali? Is that you? Oh my god!"

"Reese!" I said. "Hey. What's up?"

"Are you here? Where are you?"

"I'm..." I looked out the window. "I'm right across from you. I'm in the pool house."

"Oh my god," said Reese. "Are you serious? I'm so glad. I want to see you! Cali! The prince of Venice Beach!"

"I wanna see you too," I said back.

Her voice changed then. "You have to get away from those people. I'm in the studio. Get rid of those people and come out here." She paused for a moment. "But just you. Not them. Tell them I'll shoot if they try to follow you."

"Okay," I said.

But Darius was already shaking his head emphatically no. One of the SWAT guys was studying the studio with night-vision binoculars. The other SWAT guy, with the tranquilizer dart, was on his knees on the floor, drilling a hole through the wall.

"Actually," I said, "I'm not sure they'll let me."

"They'll let you. You just have to wait for the right moment."

Darius continued to shake his head no. I said into the phone, "They seem really serious that I can't come there."

"Let me talk to them," said Reese.

I handed the phone to Darius.

Darius took the phone. "Hello?" he said.

The room became even more quiet. Everyone leaned forward to hear what Reese would say to Darius.

"Reese?... Hello?" he said.

There was no response.

Then: a gunshot. It was loud and it shook the glass of the pool house. Everyone ducked or jumped away from the window. The guy to my left, who was guarding a side door, dove behind a chair. This was apparently the "right moment" Reese had been talking about.

I slipped to my left and tried the side door. It opened. A second later, I was outside, on the lawn, untouched.

I hurried down the grass slope toward the art studio. Again, the outside world was perfectly calm and quiet. You would not have known there was anyone on the property. A warm, light breeze drifted in off the ocean. Stars were visible in the sky.

I reached the side door of the little house and knocked.

"Who is it?" came Reese's suspicious voice.

"Cali."

"Are you alone?"

"Yes."

"If you're not I'm going to shoot."

"I'm alone."

I heard a lock turn in the door. I waited a moment, then pushed it gently with my fingertips. It opened. Slowly, I entered.

With the windows covered and no lights on, it was totally dark inside. I came in anyway, completely blind, and shut the door behind me.

"Cali?" came Reese's voice in the darkness. "Do you have a recording device or a gun or anything else hidden on you?"

"No," I said, keeping my hands out where she could see them.

"Are you trying to trick me in any way?"

"No."

My eyes were adjusting to the blackness. I could make out Reese's figure standing before me. She held a silver pistol with both hands. It was pointed at the wood floor between us. By her stance, it looked like she'd shot a gun before.

"You know about guns, don't you?" I said to her.

"A little. Enough to shoot someone."

"I've been trying to learn about guns," I said. "For my business. It seems like everyone in the world knows about guns except me."

"This used to be my grandfather's. It's Swiss, I think. I don't remember what it's called."

"Maybe you can show it to me sometime."

"It's not that hard to figure out."

It seemed so natural, this conversation. It was like we were just chatting away, like before. That's how easy it was to be with Reese. She was like my instant best friend again.

"How's your detective agency going?" she asked.

"We don't have any new cases," I said in the dark.

We both stood there, on guard, on alert, watching each other.

And then we both realized how silly that was.

"You might as well sit down," she said, lowering the gun to her side.

I could see there was an old armchair near me and moved in that direction. I sat. Reese moved the opposite direction and sat down on a small couch across the room.

"Sorry to be so paranoid," she said.

"That's okay," I said.

"Being surrounded by SWAT teams kinda does that to you."

"I'm sure it does."

"How many people are out there?"

"Quite a few," I said.

She sighed. "It's so nice to see you, though. And hear your voice."

"It's nice to see you," I said.

We sat in the darkness for a moment without speaking.

"You know why I'm here, don't you?" she said.

"No, actually, I don't."

"My mother didn't commit suicide."

I nodded in the dark. "So it was your dad then? Like you thought originally."

"No. It wasn't my dad."

There was a coldness in her voice I had never heard before. She sounded older suddenly, like a different person. Not like the Reese I knew.

"My mother," she said. "There are things I didn't tell you about her."

"Like what?" I asked.

"Things that change the situation." She sat quietly for a moment. "Do you really want to hear?"

"I do."

Reese stared down at her knees. "My mother made things possible for him. For my dad. She gave him permission in a way. To do things. To her. And to me."

I nodded, though I still didn't have a clear picture of what she was talking about.

Reese said, "I would tell her things. Things that happened. And she would look at me and she would say, 'Why are you talking about your father that way? Why would you accuse him of that? Your father loves you.' Then she would refuse to talk to me, she would leave me alone, she would go away and leave me alone in the house... with him...."

I didn't speak. I sat there.

Reese stared at the gun in her lap. She shook her head. "I should have killed *him*," she said. "I'd be a hero if I'd killed *him*." She stared thoughtfully at the drapes covering the window. "I might kill him still."

I tried to see her face in the dark, to see if this was a joke or not. "You should probably not kill anybody," I said. "If you can help it."

"Oh my god, Cali," she said with sudden brightness from the couch. "I love your sense of humor. I've really missed you."

I tried to smile at her. But it was still too dark to see her facial expression.

"So what else is happening?" she said, completely changing her tone. "How's Ailis? Are you two still partners?"

"Yeah."

"What about Strawberry?"

"She's around," I said. "She's volunteering at the animal shelter."

"Oh, that's great. I love your friends, Cali. You're all so free. I love thinking about how free you all are."

"I'm sorry about your mother," I said.

"I know," said Reese, being even more weirdly cheerful. "You know what the interesting part is? Psychologically? After my mother died, my whole personality changed. Like really changed. I turned into a completely different person. I sort of had to. I couldn't handle it, I guess."

"What did you change into?"

"The person you met. The person you helped create. A totally new, awesome person who was going to travel and be young and free and maybe live in a treehouse and go off the grid and start everything over. I was going to be the girl version of Cali. The only problem was, the whole *changing myself* thing, it didn't work. All that happened was I started to break apart. And then it started to go bad. That was when I was on the bus. Heading east. It got *so bad*. I don't even want to tell you...."

"What about your medications? Didn't they help? You seemed okay before."

"That wasn't the medication," she said. "That was you, Cali. You did that. That was your positive influence on my poor, damaged soul. That was your *innocence*. That was your *belief* in the goodness of the world."

"But if you were happy once, can't you be happy again?"

"Do you think that's possible?"

"Of course," I said. "You can get help. People want to

223

help you. That whole pool house is full of people who want to help you."

"Oh, Cali, you are the sweetest boy. You are *sooo* sweet. You always think everything is going to work out. And so for you, it always does."

Somewhere outside there was movement. I could sense it deep in my being. Someone was running or maybe a vehicle was crawling slowly over the lawn. I half expected the door to be broken down, or a tear-gas canister to come flying through the window. But neither happened.

Reese rested her head on the back of the sofa and stared dully at the wood ceiling. There were paintings I now saw, against the wall. The whole room was full of brushes and canvases and art stuff.

"You're probably getting bored," she said finally. "I'm sorry. I'm gonna fall asleep if I'm not careful."

"What are you gonna do?" I asked her.

"I think I want to talk to my father. In public. Where everyone can hear."

"You think that's a good idea?"

"I don't know. But that's what I want to do. I want to talk to him once, in the open, with the whole world as my witness."

"Well," I said, "maybe you can do that."

"I know he's up there," she said, looking in the direction of the pool house.

"He is," I said.

Reese didn't respond. A slow gray silence formed between us then. It was not like the other silences. Reese was slipping away from me in some way. I could feel it.

"If I ask you to do something," she said in a thin, airless voice, "will you swear to do it, exactly the way I say?"

"If I can."

"I'll tell you what it is, and you tell me if you can or not."

"Okay."

"I'm gonna leave this right here," she said, setting the gun on the couch. "And I'm going to walk over to you. And I want you to give me a hug. Then I want you to go back to the pool house and tell my father to come down here."

"Yeah, but you can't shoot him."

"If I promise to not shoot him, will you do the other part?"

"Of course."

"Okay then. I promise."

She left the gun on the couch and stood up. It was still very dark in the room, but I could see her straightening her shirt, smoothing her hair, composing herself.

Then she moved across the room to where I was.

Her smell reached me first. It was different somehow. And when she got closer, I saw what Darius had warned me about. There was an emptiness in her eyes. And a disconnectedness. Her whole face looked stricken and aged and strained to the point of total collapse.

She put her arms around my neck. She pressed her slightly cold body against me and pressed her face into my shoulder. I held her, cautiously at first, but then more like a real hug. It was still nice to hold her, no matter what else was happening. And she needed it now. I could feel how bad she needed it.

A wet spot formed on my shoulder. The tiniest sniffle escaped from her chest.

She lifted her head. "Thank you," she whispered. She released me and pulled away and walked back to the couch. I waited for her to turn back toward me. But she didn't. She wasn't going to. She wanted me to leave now, to fulfill my part of the bargain.

I let myself out the door. Outside, in the night air, I could feel the eyes of the police and the SWAT people on me. I headed uphill, through the grass, taking two nervous steps toward the pool house. For some reason, I couldn't catch my breath. My chest felt heavy and constricted. I stopped for a moment to gather myself.

I started again, moving uphill, one step, another step. But again I seized up. I couldn't seem to move. *Just walk to the pool house*, I told myself. *Just take another step.* It was my body that was stopping me. My body knew. My body knew what was about to happen, even if my brain did not.

A single shot rang out. It was much louder than the first one. It cleared the air like a church bell. It was such a full, complete sound. Powerful and final. And yet a moment later, it was gone, blown away by the wind, sucked into the vastness of the ocean in the distance.

The side door of the pool house swung open. I remained unable to move. Darius and his men poured out. They sprinted for the art studio. Richard Abernathy, to my surprise, was right behind them, frantic and whimpering. Other people came charging down the lawn behind them. Cops. Plainclothes. Medics. Guys with a stretcher. I stood frozen in place. Stuck in the grass. As if God himself had nailed me to the earth.

TWENTY EIGHT

"...Hello?" said a voice.

I lifted my head from my pillow. It was cold in the tree-house, one of the first chilly nights of November. I was supposed to be reading *Huckleberry Finn* for my GED class, but really, I was just lying there.

"...Cali?" said the voice.

I rolled over and pushed open my door. It was Ailis, standing in the grass below me.

It had been several months since the night at the pool house. I had not seen Ailis much during that time, except sometimes at the community college. We'd talked on the phone a little. She had mostly given me space, given me time to process everything. And of course she'd stayed with me the night of Reese's funeral, which I wasn't invited to. We'd watched a movie called *Space Visitors 3* that night, on Hope's big TV.

Lately, though, she was wondering about her own future. I couldn't really blame her.

"You know those business cards I told you about?" she said from the lawn. "Do you still want to see them?"

"Oh...uh..." I said. "Sure."

Ailis climbed the ladder. She had not been in the treehouse in a long time. We kept bumping foreheads. I managed to make a space for her to show me the business cards.

Ailis began laying them out. "Here's one option," she said, putting down the first card. It said MISSING PERSONS over a dark blue background.

"And here's another," she said, putting down a different card. It was the same thing with a light red background.

She laid eight different cards out. I looked at the possibilities. Ailis watched me, pulling her hair back behind her ear.

I pointed to the ones I liked, and the ones I didn't.

She nodded at my choices. But she could see I wasn't thinking very hard about it. I didn't care what color the business cards were.

After a while she gathered them back up. "Do you think you'll want to continue with this, in general?"

I didn't know how to answer her. I shrugged.

"I mean, there's no hurry," said Ailis.

"I know."

"But if you want, maybe I could put an ad somewhere. Just to see. On Craigslist or something."

I stared at the business cards in her hands.

"Or not..." said Ailis.

I wanted to say something. I wanted to tell Ailis how I felt, or what I wanted to do. But I didn't know.

"All right," said Ailis. She slipped her business cards back in her pocket. She looked around at the treehouse. "What do you do up here when it gets cold?"

"I get a thicker sleeping bag," I said.

The next morning, I played hoops with Diego and Jojo. This was still the best way I knew to clear my mind and think about things: to lose myself in the rhythms and flow of basketball. What was I going to tell Ailis? I owed her some sort of answer.

Jax came by later and we all walked down to the new farmer's market on Venice Boulevard. Strawberry was there, at the little animal-shelter booth. She was showing people the different dogs that needed homes. It was funny seeing Strawberry doing that. She was the one who needed a home.

Jax was nice to her, like he always was. Protective. Like a big brother. But that was it. Whatever romantic feelings that existed between them had faded, I guess. Strawbs had pulled away. She couldn't handle it.

Jax bent down and petted the dog she was holding. Strawbs watched him while he did, with those big, strange eyes of hers.

✺   ✺   ✺

Sometime after that, I had a conversation with Jojo about Reese. I didn't refer to her by name. Instead I asked him what he thought about suicide. He said it was a selfish act. An act by someone who does not trust in God. And who puts himself first, before God, and thinks he knows better.

But then, I guess he could see something in my face, and he went back to being his more usual Jojo self, saying stuff about life being a mystery, and that we must humble ourselves before forces we don't understand. And above all, we must keep our hearts open, we must always be ready to love, even though the world is full of pain and loss and sadness.

Then we went back to the basketball court and beat the crap out of these dudes from Beverly Hills, who were being jerks. It was quite satisfying.

A couple nights later, after my GED class, I was skateboarding through the parking lot and Ailis pulled up in her car. "Hey. Gotta minute?" she said. "I wanna show you something."

We drove to the Starbucks down the street. Inside, she pulled out a bunch of printouts. She began spreading them across the table.

Several of the pages were e-mails between Ailis and another person. I didn't understand at first. Then I did: Someone had responded to an ad Ailis had placed for MISSING PERSONS INCORPORATED. Someone actually wanted to hire us.

Ailis handed me the first e-mail. The man was from Hadley Creek, South Dakota. He had a daughter who had run away to California. Could we help?

In his next e-mail was some basic information about the daughter. She was fifteen. Her name was Ellie Ferguson. There was a recent picture of her standing next to a pig at a livestock fair. She was not rich. She was not pretty. In the photo, she looked bored.

I read the other e-mails. The Fergusons were divorced. Ellie lived with her dad, on their small farm. Ellie had always been the joy of Mr. Ferguson's life, but during the last year, something had happened, she'd grown distant, she would barely speak to him. When she disappeared, he searched her room and found a travel book about California stashed in her mattress. The section describing Venice had been heavily highlighted.

There were half a dozen pictures of Ellie. In one of them, she was eleven years old, standing in front of a barn in the early-morning light. She wore high rubber boots for the mud, a thick down coat for the cold. It looked just like Nebraska and for a moment I could smell the black earth, I could feel the frigid wind whipping across the plains.

"We gotta find this girl," I said softly to myself.

Ailis said nothing. But I could feel the excitement from her side of the table. And the relief.

"When did she go missing?" I asked.

"Uh…" said Ailis, digging through the e-mails. She picked one out and read it. "Eight days ago."

I nodded.

"How long did it take you to get to California?" asked Ailis.

"About a week," I said.

"Which means she could be here already," said Ailis.

I nodded and sat back and stared at the spread of papers in front of me. "Which means this case starts now."

ACKNOWLEDGMENTS

Special thanks to Bethany Strout for extreme patience and superb editorial guidance. Big thanks to Jodi Reamer, Alec Shane, Cecilia de la Campa, Kassie Evashevski, Johnny Pariseau, Lauren Cerand, Sally, Chelsea, my LA crew, and everyone who helped and supported along the way. Thanks to all the great people at Little, Brown and Writers House and UTA. Special thanks to Paula Nelson for a close reading of the manuscript when she should have been enjoying her summer. And a special acknowledgment to my good friend Mike Hughes, who first told me about life on the beach in Venice.